KNOTTY BOY

Summary of Adventures #2

Alex Silver

CONTENTS

Copyright

BLURB

I've always wanted a daddy to love me, even at my naughtiest. My reputation as a brat is one I've earned, but I wish it wouldn't scare away all my potential partners before they get to know me. I am so much more than my lack of impulse control, if only someone would stick around for longer than a scene or two.

Luke is the first person I've played with in a while who can handle me at my worst. He gets me in a way most doms don't bother trying. The only problem is, he's my best friend's brother.

With my track record, it's only a matter of time before I scare Luke away. And when the inevitable happens, I don't want to put Tate in the middle of my drama. Is it really worth risking my closest friendship for a chance at everything I've ever wanted?

Knotty Boy is a kinky M/M romance between Monty, a pudgy brat with ADHD and Luke, a rope bondage expert and daddy dom who is used to taking charge. The book contains BDSM elements including spanking, rope bondage, suspension bondage, and daddy kink. It's part of the series Summer of Adventures, but it can stand alone.

CHAPTER 1

Monty

There is nothing quite like summer sunshine after a long and dreary winter. And considering the amount of cloudy days we get in the Pacific Northwest, these bright, warm days are even more fleeting. I hate being cooped up inside during our cold Vancouver winters, so I seldom pass up a chance to get out and play. That's why, when it was my turn to plan the weekly hang out for my closest friends, I chose the beach.

The others wanted to stick to hanging out at Adventures, the kink club we all belong to. I get their point. The beach outing means we have to keep the kink tame enough for public consumption. But I can't resist the lure of playing in the sand and splashing in the water with my friends. And it's not like we don't meet up at the club often. At least once a week. Heck, Martin, the owner, even lets us play our monthly D&D sessions at the club before it opens. So when I get the chance, I want to be outside with the sun on my face and the wind in my long hair.

Tate, my best friend, is in the zone. For all he complained the loudest about my venue choice, he seems perfectly content now that we're here. He and Connor are burying Harry in the sand with some little plastic shovels from the dollar store. Harry isn't a sub like the rest of us, but when he started running our D&D campaign, we made him an honorary member of our little group.

Too bad he's not a daddy dom either. If he was, I'd hit that. He's got muscle for days from hauling lumber and operating tools. And possibly the gym. He looks like he could toss me around without quibbling over my size.

Then again, his vanilla tendencies might be just as well. Harry's a good friend and fucking him might make our game nights awkward when the fling inevitably runs its course. I sigh, stretching out on my towel and soaking up the sun after my swim.

The only thing that would make today better would be if I had a daddy to slather on my sunscreen and fuss over me. Make me wear my hat and compliment the cute dinosaurs on my new swim trunks. Maybe spank me afterward if I deserved it. And let's face it, I pretty much always earn a spanking.

Quent is the only one of us who currently has a partner. Their domme, Kylee, didn't come with us today. That doesn't stop Quent from digging in the dirt and playing the pup in subtle ways. Nothing that would draw too much attention from passersby, but enough to make us all laugh. I love playing with them at Adventures when we have little nights.

It's always nice to play, and pretend I have a daddy for keeps when I catch a dom's eyes for an evening. Or, heck, even just a dom or domme who's willing to play. I'm not too picky about my temporary partners' gender if it means I get to scene with a big. I'm almost always up for a funishment. And that goes double for getting tied up if I can find an amenable partner.

Thoughts of ropes remind me of Luke. He joined Adventures recently. I know he's a daddy dom, but he's also a rigger. And I've been fantasizing about getting him to top me since the first time I saw him doing his thing at a workshop ages ago.

When he first stepped foot in the club, I thought it was my lucky night. And then Tate had dashed my hopes when he pointedly got up and left the room at the sight of Luke. Turns out, he's actually Tate's step-brother. And Luke appearing at the club had taken Tate by surprise. They usually try to give each other space when they play, but Adventures has more queer members than any other club in the area after the place Luke used to go closed. So they agreed to share the club and just stay out of each other's way. All that is a long way to say I shouldn't want Luke.

Tate is my best friend. Ergo, sleeping with his brother would be wrong, step or not. Which might be a part of the allure, if I'm honest. Not the fact it would hurt Tate. That's the part that's holding me back. It's the naughtiness of the idea that calls to my bratty side. The part that revels in trying to get away with something I shouldn't. Too bad Luke isn't here today. On the rare occasions we're both at the club, I enjoy flirting with him until I can practically see his palm itching to spank away my attitude.

I flop onto my belly to sun my back and hide my erection. The warm day is a perfect preview of the lazy summer I have planned. Nothing can beat getting to relax while my friends play in the sand nearby. Well, nothing except having my dream daddy here, too. I let myself indulge in thinking about Luke's hands on my body, tying me up and making me not at all sorry I disobeyed.

CHAPTER 2

Luke

Adventures hosts little nights twice a month. So far, I've stayed away on these nights, to let Tate have his space with his friends. But I've been hoping to find a boy to satisfy my daddy dom urges for a while now. It's why I joined Adventures after my old club closed. That was before I realized my step-brother was among the littles who attend regularly. Some things neither of us needed to learn about the other's sex life. But the cat is out of the bag. And it's not that weird to play in the same space now that the initial surprise has worn off.

Heck, learning Tate is a little who craves a daddy dom's care will always rank as less weird than our moms' engagement dinner. I doubt anything will beat the weirdness of being introduced to my new step-brother when we were both seventeen, only to recognize him as my summer camp blow job buddy. Talk about awkwardness. We haven't fooled around since finding out our moms are in love. Too complicated, and the fling we shared was all about convenience and teenage hormones. In hindsight, it's sort of funny that our sexual interests line up so well.

But, it's not like I strictly scene as a daddy. I've had no shortage of partners asking to be tied up since joining Adventures. I got into ropes to make myself more desirable as a dom, at first. When I got past the basics, I discovered how much I enjoyed being a rigger.

Val, a regular at my old kink club, took me under her wing to teach me more over the past several years. What that woman can do with rope is nothing short of art.

I've learned enough that my skills are popular. Mostly, I've obliged the folks at Adventures who want to play with me. To where I sometimes feel like a fair ride that everyone wants to try. Variety is the spice of life and I'm not actively looking for anything permanent.

Sure, it would be nice to be wanted for more than a night with my ropes, but I'll take what I can get. If that's being a novelty for a single scene, then I still get laid most nights that I hit the club. And I have no shortage of folks willing to play with me, with or without sex being part of the scene.

It's a pity that Martin, the owner, hasn't got a proper setup for suspension work or a suitable space to set up a portable frame. At least I have some solid hard points installed at home, so I can keep in practice. With all the requests I get, it would be fun to do a suspension demo here.

More often than not, I come to Adventures to play with my ropes. Tonight, though, Tate had an emergency call out for work. He texted to let me know I've got free rein to check out the littles playing in the public play area of the club without intruding on his play time.

And the minute I walk in, there's Tate's best friend, Monty. He's letting Quent suck him off in front of Quent's domme. Kylee is petting Quent and telling them what a good pup they are, while Monty begs for more.

I take a moment to appreciate the scene playing out before me. Monty lays sprawled on a vinyl beanbag chair, legs akimbo, to make room for Quent. He has his head thrown back to expose his throat and his arms wrapped around a stuffy like it's the only thing keeping him grounded.

Kylee pulls Quent off Monty's dick and Quent sets to licking all over Monty's groin, ignoring the boy's shiny condom-clad erection in favor of teasing him. Club rules mandate condoms for any sex acts. Kylee's got a devious streak, making the notoriously bratty Monty beg for release.

Monty has caught my eye before. He's got a magnetic personality and striking long red hair. The fantasy of wrapping that long silky queue around my fist to hold him in place while I fuck his smart mouth has tempted me more than once. Until tonight, the potential fallout of a one-nighter with my brother's best friend didn't seem worth the risk, though. Tonight, there's something about watching him clutch a stuffed dog to his chest while one of his friends slobbers all over his cock without actually sucking him off that has me giving him a closer look.

There's another reason I've steered clear of the boy. Brats are not my kink, and Monty's reputation precedes him, no matter how often I catch him giving me and my ropes longing looks from across the club. Willful disobedience doesn't do it for me, most of the time.

I suspect it's only loyalty to Tate that keeps him from approaching me. It's why I haven't scened with any of the littles in his close friend group. Watching Monty now has me second guessing whether he might be worth ruffling Tate's feathers over.

I wander closer, drawn to the scene. Kylee catches my eye and nods in greeting, without interrupting the scene between boy and pup. I've tied up her pup before. Quent responded beautifully to the bondage, letting it sweep them away to subspace while Kylee and I teamed up to tease them with sensation play before we both fucked the pup.

Domme and pup both seemed excited about having me join them for a spit roast. Q has a talented mouth and Kylee pegged the pup just right so that they writhed against the cradling ropes, moaning and caught between my dick and their mommy's strap-on.

Since the scene took place in the privacy of my personal play area, I had zero qualms about joining in. Public sex isn't my favorite way to play. I'd rather an audience admire my rope work than have my dick on display. Being exposed in the middle of the club is something Kylee has no problem with, she's stroking herself as she directs Quent's interaction with Monty.

Monty has no problem with having an audience for his orgasms either. This isn't the first time I've seen his dick. It's only unusual in that, more often than not, he's the one getting fucked or giving head. He looks strangely vulnerable on display like this, helpless and being pleasured out of his mind. It makes me wonder how he'd look dangling from my ceiling while my dick drives into that delectable ass. Then Monty's eyes flutter open and he sees me watching him. The boy gives me a dreamy smile, lifting one hand and waggling his fingers at me in greeting.

"That's my good pup. Time to finish playing with Monty so you can have your treat," Kylee instructs.

Quent's entire ass waggles with excitement as they dive onto Monty's latex covered dick to finish sucking him off. Monty jackknives upright as he moans Quent's name, eyes shut and mouth slack as he comes into his friend's eager mouth.

Quent makes a self-satisfied sound around the dick in their mouth. They suckle on Monty a little longer before pulling off and licking Monty on the mouth, very much like an affectionate canine companion.

That makes Monty laugh as he hugs his friend around the neck. "Good puppy." He releases Quent, deals with the used condom, and reaches for his discarded jockstrap. "Thanks for playing with me, Miss Kylee."

"You are very welcome, Monty. Q loves having a tasty bone to play with, don't you pup?"

Quent nods and nuzzles into their domme's crotch, mouthing at Kylee's groin like they would happily go down on her next, if she let them. Kylee ruffles the pup's hair and presses them closer in encouragement. "That's a good pup. Let's go see if the exam room is available. You're due for a vet check, aren't you?"

Quent whines as Kylee pushes their head away.

"Enough, get your toy, or you'll be late; you don't want to keep the vet waiting, pup." Kylee insists. Monty holds up the well-loved stuffy and Quent snatches it between their teeth. Then the pup lets their mommy lead them away to the private room where Martin has a faux-medical setup available.

Monty slumps back in the beanbag chair and sets about wriggling into his jockstrap.

"Did you come to play tonight?" Monty asks me, his hopeful smile is utterly transparent. The boy wants me.

"I did." I nod, watching him tuck himself away. The jockstrap has a dinosaur monogrammed over his bulge. Cute.

"Because Tate isn't here?" Monty tugs at his shirt, drawing my attention to the monster emblazoned over his chest. More often than not, Monty wears cute graphic tees and booty shorts to the club. Tonight, the caption under the monster reads 'Daddy's little monster'. It makes my heart ache for him. I might not come to little nights often, but I've seen enough of Monty to guess the slogan is aspirational. He doesn't have a daddy dom of his own.

"Yeah. Work emergency. He texted to say I should come since he can't."

"Would you play with me?" Monty asks, pouting out his lip and giving me his best puppy-dog eyes.

I run a hand through my hair, considering all the reasons this is a terrible idea, then I decide, what the heck. It's one night, not a lifetime commitment. "Sure, Monty. What would you like to play?"

He bounces up out of his seat to grab my hand and drag me over to a table where some littles are coloring. "Let's draw! You can tell me how good my pictures are." He tugs my fingers, eager to get to the fun.

"Can I?" I try to stifle my amusement. I love the bubbly energy of playing with a little and the way they crave gentle guidance.

"You can. Monty nods as he grabs a coloring sheet with a pony on it and gets to work coloring outside the lines. Of course he's a handful. Is he testing to see if I'll praise his work no matter what, or does he want me to suggest he stay in the lines? I've played with both kinds of little before.

I sidestep the issue for now, sitting and watching him color with his tongue caught between his teeth. "Why did you decide on purple for the grass, Monty?"

"It's Alpha Centauri. The Centaurs eat purple grass. That's why their hooves are purple."

"And is that a centaur?" I point to the stick figure person he drew in dark purple after scribbling out the head and neck of the pony.

"Yep." He holds the picture up proudly. "See, and that's me and my daddy riding the centaur." He points out two more scribbled stick people.

"Yeah?"

"Yep. Want to keep it?" He fixes me with the most hopeful pleading expression, like taking his picture is some wonderful treat.

"Sure, Monty." I make a show of examining the artwork. "I love it."

"Um, Daddy? Wait, sorry, can I call you Daddy for tonight?"

"You may."

Monty beams at me and launches himself to hug me around the neck. "Awesome. Thanks, Daddy. I'm bored with coloring. Can we do something else?"

"Like what?" I ask, gently easing out of his embrace.

"I don't know." He rocks back on his heels, and I suspect he knows exactly what he wants to do. "You could tie me up and make me fly like an airplane. Quent says they've never experienced anything like it."

"Unfortunately, the club doesn't have the right set up for that." I gesture around the room.

"You could take me home and tie me up there." He cajoles.

"Not tonight, Monty."

"Fine." He pouts at me, snatching his picture out of my hands and tearing it in half. "Then you can't have my picture."

This sort of tantrum I know how to handle. I've seen Monty in action before. Not in little mode, but playing the brat with other doms. The boy loves being spanked. "That was very naughty. You gave me that picture, Monty. It was mine, and you ruined it."

"So what?" he puffs out his chest and crosses his arms.

"So, naughty boys get punished." I nod toward one of the low benches in the play area. Monty has a voyeuristic streak, as I already saw this evening. He enjoys having an audience when he gets spanked, too. So I'm pretty sure he'll agree to this, even if his contrary nature drives him to fight it every step of the way. Giving him a command I know he'll enjoy following seems like a safe bet to get him to fall in line.

"You're not my daddy." He scowls and turns his back on me, jutting out his chin in defiance. He's cute as hell when he pouts.

His angry words have his usual attitude behind them, but there's a longing there, too. One I recognize because I suspect he wants a daddy to love him as much as I want to find my perfect boy. That might not be Monty long-term, but we can meet each other's needs for the night.

"I'm not, but you asked to play with me. So for tonight, I can be the one to punish my naughty boy. If you want." I reason with him. This conversation works better than him capitulating right away. Even though I know Monty's general likes and dislikes, I'd rather hear him ask me specifically for anything we do in a scene. God, that ass of his is perfectly fuckable, and framed by the jock. Monty is chubby, and I want to pinch his jiggly cheeks. "A spanking?" Monty perks up at the offer, turning toward me.

"If you want." I shrug, like it doesn't matter to me if he agrees. It does. I want him, and it's rare for him to come to the club when Tate isn't around.

"In front of everyone?" he demands, licking his lips and taking in the crowd with a calculating gleam in his eyes. Greedy boy, I've got him hooked.

"Yes." I stifle a smile, since I'm supposed to be punishing him. With Monty, these scenes are definitely more funishment since the boy enjoys it so much.

"Will you fuck me after?" Monty presses his luck. Typical Monty.

"In one of the private rooms. I don't fuck in public."

"Okay." Monty nods and tugs me toward the bench I suggested using.

"Okay, what?" I arch a brow at him, refusing to be budged.

"Okay, Daddy." Monty rolls his eyes. "I'll be your naughty boy and you can spank me and then drag me to a private room to fuck my brains out."

"Such a needy naughty boy, aren't you?" I cluck my tongue at him.

"Yes. I'm very naughty." He skips off toward the bench. "Come punish me, Daddy."

I can't help smiling at his irrepressible attitude despite my usual reservations about brats as I follow the boy.

CHAPTER 3

Monty

Daddy Luke sits on the bench while I dance from foot to foot, impatient to get to the fun already. I'm going to blow all over his lap if I can't cool off, but damn. Luke makes me hard. I've fantasized about a scene like this with him so many times, it's like it's hard-wired into my psyche. I rub at my dick with the base of my palm.

"Naughty boys don't get to touch their dicks, Monty." Daddy Luke reaches out to stop me. His grip on my wrist, gentle but firm, makes me shiver in delight.

"Sorry, Daddy. I'll be good," I promise, trying to look contrite now that I've won my prize.

"I'm sure you will." He pats his lap. "You can keep the jock on. We're using the club safewords. Tell me what they are."

"Red, yellow and green, Daddy." I try to be at least a little obedient, so I don't lose out on my treat. He wouldn't be the first Daddy I proved to be too much for before we even get to the good stuff. I wait to see how he wants me.

"Good boy. Lay across my thighs, please." Daddy pats his lap in invitation. Jackpot, some of my previous play partners have told me I'm too big for this, but it's still my favorite position for taking a spanking. It seems more intimate this way. I don't hesitate before I drape myself over him, humping against his leg a little, just to get a rise out of Daddy. Being good is hard.

"Dick between my legs, not rubbing against me, naughty boy." Daddy Luke swats my thigh gently in rebuke. Mm, the first taste of the familiar sting makes me happy. I can't wait until he gets to the actual spanking.

I wriggle into position, enjoying the way his hard bulge presses against my belly when I slide forward. Good. He likes me, too. Even at my brattiest.

When I'm where he wants me, Daddy Luke brings his palm down on my ass in a series of three sharp cracks. I can't help trying to rub against him at the rush of sensation. Too bad there's nothing but air under my groin. I moan. Daddy moves to the other cheek, giving me a few more smacks. Then he switches to alternating cheeks. After several stinging blows, he stops to let the heat and sting build. I squirm, wriggling my ass to entice him to hit me again.

"You want more, Monty?" Daddy sounds amused as I lift my ass toward him.

"Yes, please, Daddy."

"Do you know why Daddy is spanking you?"

"Because I'm naughty." Oh, great, let's dissect my lack of impulse control, just what I need when I'm playing. I hate reciting my list of sins. I just want to float away on sensation.

That flippant reply nets me another gentle swat, more tease than actual spank. "Details, boy."

"I tore up your picture that I made you. And I was mouthy."

"You, my boy, are always mouthy, aren't you?" Daddy Luke reaches around me to grip my face, pushing a finger past my lips.

I suck on his fingertip for a second, and then I nip him gently with my teeth. Typical me, ruining a good thing with my inability to resist the urge to act out every foolish impulse that flits through my head. Daddy Luke jerks his hand back and I get another few swats on the ass. Guess he can't be too mad if he's using that as a punishment. Or else he's so mad he forgot just how much I enjoy being spanked.

In any case, I revel in the rain of smacks lighting up my ass and making my dick ache with need. Tears sting my eyes. I press my face against his calf and groan as he gets me to the sweet spot. That magical mental place where I'm just floating above the sting as each new spank blends into the previous one and my entire ass starts to burn and throb. He stops, then grabs both my ass cheeks and massages them roughly with his palms, reigniting the ache in every nerve ending all over again.

Daddy Luke's got me gasping and rutting against him. Oh fuck, that hurts so good. I want more. Want him to give me more. What I wouldn't give not to have this scene end. Not ever. I wish he was really my daddy. The deep-seated yearning makes a sob catch in my throat and tears streak my face.

"Sorry, Daddy," I sob.

"I know you are." Daddy Luke soothes me, his hands on my ass turn gentle, caressing me. Then he adds, "good boys don't bite." Daddy Luke punctuates each word with another hard spank. The sudden shift from soft comfort back to punishment makes me gasp and grind against him more. I'm all snot-faced from crying, unable to help the response.

"I'm not a good boy, Daddy," I admit, voice tearful from crying, but not at all contrite.

Daddy Luke lifts me up, maneuvering me around to sit on his lap. I wince at the initial zing of renewed burn from sitting on my sore ass. Once the first blush of pain recedes, I shimmy in place to reignite the sensation and hopefully drive Daddy Luke wild, too. He wraps his arms around me, tucking my face against his chest and wiping away my tears.

"I wouldn't say that, Monty. You're being a very good naughty boy for me tonight."

"That makes no sense." I sniffle into his chest, since he doesn't seem to mind me being a snotty mess all over him.

"You like to act out and get punished for it, right?" Daddy Luke rubs soothing circles on my back while I get my crying under control. It's a much needed emotional release, and a big part of the reason I like to play this way.

"Yeah."

"And I understood that when I agreed to play with you tonight. So you did exactly what we both wanted. I'd say that makes you a wonderful boy." He doesn't stop touching me even when I'm out of tears.

"Even though what I did was bad?"

"Yep."

"So, does that mean you're still going to fuck me?" I wriggle hopefully against his bulge.

"If you still want me to." Daddy Luke presses his bulge against my sore ass and I moan and grind down on him, making him chuckle. Some daddies I've played with aren't into sex when I'm in little mode. I get it, but I'm still an adult, regardless of how I'm acting, and I enjoy sex. Especially with someone who isn't afraid to punish me and fuck me. Plus, unlike my friends, I don't typically regress that far into little space most of the time. It's not the true allure of this type of play for me. I enjoy being cared for and not having to worry about anything but the moment.

"Yes, please, Daddy Luke." I put on my best manners. Tate jokes that I'm more of a horny middle than a little, which I always tell him is silly. I don't care if I'm acting five or fifteen. I don't bother arguing too hard with Tate because the details of it all don't matter to me as much as having a safe space to act uninhibited. That, and finding someone to take care of me, even if it's only for the length of an evening.

"Get up, and let's go find a private room, then." Daddy Luke pats my hips to encourage me to get up. I stand, wobbling at being upright after my spanking. Daddy Luke steadies me and guides me to one of the available rooms where we can fuck.

The one he chooses is simple, and I know the closed cabinet is full of all kinds of delicious toys that he could use to paddle my ass. Several crops, floggers, and paddles, some with slats and various textures to vary the impact from thuddy to stingy.

"Want to be cuffed to the bench, boy?" Luke offers. He rings my wrists with his hands in emphasis.

"No, Daddy." I tug my hands free so I can settle myself on the bench. "I just want you to hold me down and pound into me." Unable to tear my gaze away from what I'd really like, I give him my honest answer.

If the spanking was good, and it was, how much more fun could we have with the smorgasbord of sensation I know is hanging just out of reach? I try not to stare too wistfully at the closed cabinet as Luke arranges me to his liking on the padded bench. He leans me back against the reclined backrest with my ass tilted up to about his groin level and propped right at the edge of the seat. He lifts my feet up into the bench's stirrups, forcing me to spread my thighs and giving him better access to my junk.

"Do you see something you like, boy?" He notices my wistful staring, anyway. His low chuckle as he tugs on my neatly queued hair draws my gaze back to him. He's even more handsome up close. Nice chiseled jaw, buzzed hair that will bristle pleasantly if he lets me rub my fingers through it.

I'm a sucker for the soft prickle of short hair under my hands. Especially if I'm feeling it while my daddy edges me with his mouth. Arching up into him and knowing I'm not allowed to come is sweet torture. I can imagine how it would feel right now. His firm hands gripping my ass, still aching from my spanking. Squeezing and teasing and making me squirm and beg until he fills me up. It doesn't even matter which end he sticks his cock in; I just want to make him come. With another sigh, I try to wait patiently for him to decide what comes next. I need to learn to take what I can get and be content.

"You, Daddy." I bat my eyes at him, trying to look innocent.

"Oh, so you weren't ogling all Martin's impact toys?" He gestures at the cabinet that I was all but eye fucking.

"No, Daddy." I shake my head and try to plaster on a wide-eyed, innocent expression.

"Are you lying to me, boy?" He grips the back of my neck and gives me a gentle shake.

"No, Daddy. I can't see them since they're still in the cabinet."

He laughs at that. "Loopholes, mouthy boy?"

"Yes."

"Are you trying to earn a paddling before I fuck you, boy?"

"Maybe?" I tease.

"You could just ask for what you want." His exasperated words don't match his amused tone, so I give him a bit of honesty.

"I am, Daddy." I squirm. It's weird to be truly vulnerable with someone. Let him see a piece of me through the bratty antics I'm known for at the club. Daddy Luke's smile softens to something sweet and sympathetic. Like he understands what I'm not saying. That this is the only way I know how to ask. That it's easier to court rejection with outbursts than it is to be rejected for who I am and what I want.

"Did you prep before playtime, Monty?"

"Yes, Daddy." Hope springs eternal. I always clean out before little play nights.

"Show me?"

"See?" I grin at him as I spread my legs wider and reach down to part my ass cheeks with my fingers to show him my hole. Daddy Luke smiles and strokes himself.

"Get that tight little hole nice and ready for Daddy, boy." He tosses a packet of lube from the basket in reception onto my belly and I waste no time tearing it open and slicking my fingers to prep myself. Daddy Luke walks away instead of watching me. Boo. He goes behind me to shuck off his pants and roll on the condom, judging from the sounds of it. Total let down. Until he walks back around and watches me work a third finger into my ass. The extra prep is more for show than any genuine need to continue stretching muscles that are more than accustomed to a good hard fuck.

He's got one of my favorite paddles in his hand. When he notices me staring at it as I pump my fingers into my ass, he smacks it gently against his palm.

"Do you want this, Monty?"

"Yes, Daddy." I nod eagerly.

"I can tell." He nudges my very erect dick with the edge of the paddle, then gives me a few gentle taps with the flat of the head along my shaft. Oh, fuck. The threat of the pain I'd experience if he really hit me there makes my balls all tight and my dick tingly and ready to blow. I don't think I'd actually like that much pain, but knowing I'm at my daddy's mercy if he wanted to dish it out does things to me. Arousing things. I still my fingers, leaving only the tips in my ass. I can't take another thrust of my fingers without coming now that he's playing with my dick and I don't want to blow until he's inside me.

"You interested in cock and ball torture, Monty?" Daddy Luke meets my gaze, pressing the paddle against my balls and mashing them into my body, just enough to be uncomfortable. I let my fingers slip out of my ass so I can focus on what he's doing between my legs.

"Sometimes, Daddy." I lick my lips, unsure if I want him to hurt me or fuck me more. Probably both. I lift into the pressure, but he moves back, refusing to actually crush me. Probably for the best. CBT isn't really my jam, but I'd consider it for the right daddy.

"Perhaps another time, when we've discussed it before you're reduced to being a horny little monster."

"Yes, Daddy." I agree. Holy shit, he wants to play again. I could cry at that. I almost do. But then he lifts the paddle off my balls and brings it down in a hard arc that connects with my ass and outer thigh. I hiss out a breath and then moan as the sting blooms. "Oh, god, yes. Daddy, more. Please?" I beg as he rubs a palm over the spreading ache.

"Turn over, ass up and ready for me." Daddy Luke waits while I scramble up to kneel on the bench, hugging the back support I was leaning on before. I lift my ass up toward him, ready for whatever he has planned.

"See? You're a very good boy, Monty." Daddy Luke leans in close, kissing the small of my back. Then he straightens and paddles me until I'm a breathless, begging puddle of goo and my entire ass is on fire. It must be red as a tomato by now.

I'm floating somewhere far away when he pushes inside of me, but the pleasure of his dick hitting me just right breaks through the haze and grounds me. I babble every thought that flits through my head as he fucks me, begging him for more and harder.

"Oh, fuck, Daddy. Love you. This. Love this." I correct myself.

Because I don't love him after one play session. But I do love the way he's making me fly without even leaving the ground and everything he did with me tonight. I love the idea of being somebody's good naughty boy. I love that he sees me underneath my recalcitrant attitude. And I love being fucked. Love the hard, unrelenting thrusts as he seeks his release inside of me.

"Harder, fucking pound me, Daddy." I ride back to meet his thrusts. Pleasure from his dick inside me swirls together with the zinging heat of his hips meeting my ass every time he bottoms out, bringing our bodies flush. His fingers dig into my sore thighs, adding another layer to the delicious torture of competing nerve endings.

"Such a good boy, Monty, almost there. You gonna take everything I give you, boy?"

"Yes, Daddy," I gasp as he reaches around to stroke my dick. His firm strokes remain unrelenting until I spill all over his hand, bucking wildly back against him. And then he finds another gear, pressing me down onto the bench and driving in hard and fast until he comes, too. It's almost too much, him thrusting hard while I'm riding the tail end of my orgasm. But he stops before he pushes me too far.

I'm a boneless puddle when he pulls out and deals with the condom. The sounds of him tidying up the room and disinfecting the paddle he used on me are distant as I lay there, spent and floating. He lets me come down slowly from the high. Then his firm hands are on me again, cleaning me up and rubbing a cool lotion into my tender ass and thighs. I sigh contentedly. I could lay here all night with him fussing over me, but Daddy Luke eventually coaxes me up to my feet.

"Come on, I'll get you a drink and we can cuddle until you're up to going home."

"M'kay, Daddy," I agree, too happy that I still get to call him that for now to get upset about the reminder that this perfect evening will end. And when it does, I'll have to go home without him. I'm in no mood to argue. I haven't been this well fucked in ages and I could float away again if he let me. He doesn't, but he doesn't burst my happy little bubble of endorphins either. I feel sort of like a balloon, bobbing along on a string after him as he leads me to find an out of the way corner in the public play area.

Daddy Luke finds a free couch and installs me on it with a blanket. I pout when he walks away, feeling very sorry for myself. But he comes back with my favorite purple Gatorade and snuggles in next to me, urging me to lean against him as I sip my drink. And I let go of all my worries and cares while he holds me tight and murmurs about how good I was for him.

CHAPTER 4

Luke

Friday nights at Adventures are always a treat. Tate is here tonight, but we've agreed to just stay out of each other's way at general club events like this. Besides, I'm scheduled for a rope demo on the main stage this evening, so if anyone is stepping on toes, it's him. Even if he missed out on his little time two weeks ago.

My step-brother's presence is a good sign that his best friend came tonight, too. I catch myself scanning the crowd for Monty. His bright tees stand out among the more common kink and fetish wear most of the members are sporting. Lots of bare skin accented by harnesses, corsets, and jocks. Most of the folks in street clothes stick to neutral colors. But not Monty. The boy's wardrobe screams for attention as much as his behavior. It's working on me, too. Ever since our scene together last Tuesday, I can't seem to get him out of my head.

How his well-spanked ass practically glowed as I slid inside of him. The way he lifted into each spank, eager to take everything I dished out to him. His hopeful expression when I talked about seeing him again. The desperate words that had spilled from his mouth as he lost control.

I know he doesn't actually love me, not after one scene. I

pretended not to notice his slip of the tongue when we were fucking. It's clear he loves to be taken in hand by his daddy, that it gives him something he needs. I have no doubt he fantasizes about having a daddy of his own to love him and show him off at the club. So that was probably something straight out of his fantasies, more than a reflection of how he feels about me.

The boy is brimming over with the need for approval, despite doing his best not to earn it with most of his play partners. He pushes and pushes and tries to find the breaking point to drive them away. Like how he nipped my fingers when I was playing with his mouth. I don't doubt that he'd have gotten all bratty with me in the private room if I hadn't distracted him with the pain he craves. Instead of letting him push my buttons, I'd used what I knew of the boy to take him apart and he was glorious when he let go and flew.

There he is now, talking to Martin. I turn my steps toward them. I should check in with Martin, anyway. To confirm the details for my rope demo. Martin seems distracted, eyes scanning the room while they chat.

As I watch them interact, Monty lowers his gaze, like he's trying to be a good submissive. I snort. That boy struggles to submit on a good day and everyone at Adventures knows it.

If I had to guess, Monty is probably angling to get Martin to whip him. He's done demos with how to use a single tail and related safety concerns. Damn, the mental image of Monty bound and taking a lashing does it for me. I can just picture my boy desperately humping the air, or perhaps the St. Andrew's Cross in the red room as the whip bites into his back. The slow build driving him wild with need. I pull up short at that thought.

Monty isn't my anything. He's a boy I played with once. We had a good time, but that hardly makes him mine. I shake my head at my foolishness and approach Martin and Monty.

When I reach them, Monty is pouting, so I suspect he got turned down for his offer to play. It's no wonder he turned Monty down, considering that Martin is wearing an armband to indicate he's a dungeon monitor tonight. The boy ought to have known better than to ask. Not that knowing better has ever stopped Monty.

"Hey, Martin, just wanted to confirm you have me scheduled for ten, with Angel?"

Martin winces. "About that."

"Oh no, did we double book the main stage?" Calling the makeshift platform in the far corner a stage is a generous descriptor, but the club makes up for the outdated finishes with the people. Martin has built an inclusive and safe play area for his club patrons to let loose. It would be outstanding if he can actually make good on the upgrades I've heard him mention longingly on occasion since I joined.

"No, the stage is yours, such as it is." Martin grimaces. "Angel called to ask me to pass along the message that their daughter has a broken arm, so they are at the ER getting a cast. They can't make it tonight. They called the club, since they couldn't get a hold of you earlier."

"Oh no. My phone died, so I missed their call. Hopefully Bethany gets well soon. I'm sure I can find a willing victim to demonstrate with me in Angel's place tonight."

"That's what I told them, not to worry and to focus on the kiddo," Martin agrees. "Do you want me to put the word out that you need a volunteer?"

"No, I can take care of it. Thanks for passing along the message." I wave off his offer. Martin has enough going on without trying to organize things for me. I saw a few of my favorite rope bunnies in the crowd tonight. I'll have no shortage of volunteers if I ask around.

"Great, thanks for agreeing to show us the ropes." Martin winks at me. He's not a daddy dom, but he's a total dad with the corny jokes and a teenage daughter at home. He also has a habit of trying to take care of everyone who walks into his club. "Oh, Darla's signaling for me." Martin raises his hand toward a middle-aged couple standing across the room. "I think she and Dani were planning a breath play scene later tonight, once the crowd thins out. She wanted me to be on hand for it, so I should go check in with her. You're all set for the demo?"

"Yep." I nod. "My bag is in the locker room for later."

"Great, I'll talk to you both later, then." Martin claps me on the shoulder, nods toward Monty, and goes to talk to Darla.

Monty bounces on his toes beside me, eyes bright with interest. "Oh, me, please, Daddy? Pick me to be your volunteer?" He raises his hand like he's back in middle school and that gets a chuckle out of me.

"You want me to show everyone what you look like trussed up like a Christmas ham, Monty?" I tease. He wouldn't be my first choice for a demo. The boy is far from obedient. That might be fun for a scene, but not when I'm trying to show people how to do something with my attention split between my sub and the audience. It's less than ideal.

Then again, tonight is just a demo of what I can do to raise interest for a workshop later in the month. My having fun with Monty on stage might entice people to want to sign up for the workshop. And hopefully Angel, who is the picture of compliance and a total rope bunny, will be free to model at the workshop, as planned. That's when I actually have to interact with the people watching us without having to worry about a naughty boy causing trouble.

"Yes, please, Daddy." Monty giggles. "That's practically my name."

I frown. "Christmas?"

"Ham. My mom named me Hammond, after her dad. It was not

fun being the fat kid on the playground with a name like that." He shudders theatrically. "Hence I go by Monty."

"I'm sorry, Monty. I wasn't implying anything about your size." It hadn't even occurred to me he was self-conscious about it. The boy isn't body shy. At least, not that I've seen at the club. It might help that Adventures has a well-enforced zero tolerance policy about any sort of body shaming.

"No, I know you wouldn't say anything like that, Daddy." He stares down at his feet, though, shuffling in place. His shoulders hunch. "Sorry. I mean Luke."

"You can call me Daddy if you want, Monty. And I mean it, you're perfect as you are, naughty boy." I resist the urge to tip up his chin and make him realize how serious I am. Monty is still a pudgy boy, and it suits him. He's sexy the way he is, love handles that make it easy to grab hold of him and plow into him. His full, plump ass that can take a hard spanking and follow up with a rough fuck. The warm, sleepy weight of him pressing against me as he came down from the adrenaline of our scene.

"Your good naughty boy, right, Daddy?" Monty peeks up at me through his lashes, so hopeful that there's no way I can deny him anything right now.

"That's right. Daddy's good, naughty boy." I smile and tug on his pretty red hair.

"So, can I be your model tonight?" He bounces on his toes again.

"Can you be a good obedient boy up on the stage?"

He bites his lip and shakes his head. "Probably not, but I'll try my best."

"That's all I'd ever ask. Do you mind going shirtless so I can tie a harness and show you off?"

"That's fine, Daddy."

"Good. Meet me in the locker room at quarter to ten, so we can go over what I'm planning."

"It's too bad there aren't hardpoints here," he says wistfully.

"What would you want me to do with you if there were?"

"Make me fly? I could hang upside down while you fuck and spank me. Spidey-sex." He licks his lips lasciviously.

"Do all your fantasies include a spank and a fuck?" I tease him.

He considers for a long moment, stroking his chin theatrically as though it actually requires thought, then nods. "Yep, pretty much all of them, Daddy."

"Well, I'm sorry to disappoint you, but there is no spanking on the agenda for tonight." I don't intend to budge on that point, but then his lip pouts out and my mouth goes on without thinking it through, because I'm a total sucker for him. "Not as part of the demo, anyway."

"Does that mean you'd spank me after?" He sounds so hopeful. No backing out now.

"If you're a very good boy, we'll see about that. And we can talk about having you come by my place to try suspension some time, too."

"I'll be so good!" Monty nods like a bobblehead. "Thank you!"

"You are very welcome." I don't try to hide my amusement at his antics.

That must encourage him. This time, when he bounces up on his toes, Monty gloms onto my shoulder and leans in to kiss my cheek "You're the best, Daddy. See you at quarter to!" He bounces off into the crowd, making a beeline to my brother, probably to dish about getting to be tied up tonight. I watch him go with my hand pressed to my cheek where I fancy I can still feel the warmth of his lips lingering. That boy is trouble with a capital T. And I want more of him.

***

Monty gets to the locker room before me. Right on time. He's already shucking off his shirt when I open the door to get my stuff organized. I smile at him when he whirls around to see who is entering the room. He smiles back.

"Hi, Daddy. You said to lose the shirt, right?" he asks as he pulls open his locker.

"I did. Since when are you so obedient?" I tease.

"Um, since tonight, I guess." Monty's smile drops in wattage and he shrugs. Shit, that was the wrong thing to say. I meant it as a light joke. He's always making silly jokes alluding to his bratty streak, but obviously I missed the mark. "I'm sorry, that was rude of me, Monty." I step closer to him.

He shrugs again, shoulders hunching inward as he crumples up his shirt into a tight little ball. "It's the truth. Ask anyone."

"Perhaps that's half the problem. How are you supposed to succeed if we all expect you to fail? It wasn't fair for me to assume you would mess up. You've been nothing but good for me."

"Ha! Last time we played, I bit you, threw a tantrum, and destroyed your things. Even if the thing in question was only a stupid picture. And I mouth off and talk out of turn too often to keep track." He stuffs the wadded up shirt into the back of his locker and shuts the door on it.

"The picture wasn't stupid, Monty. You gave it to me and that isn't something I take lightly, okay?"

"Okay." He scuffs his toe against the ground like a kid enduring yet another pointless lecture over his behavior. I don't like seeing him sullen and dispirited. Half of what draws me to him is his energy and brightness.

"Listen. I have a rule about bringing up the past when I play with a partner." I reach for his hand and he lets me take it and give a little reassuring squeeze.

"You do?" He turns to watch me.

"I do." I nod. "Once a transgression has been discussed and punished, we don't bring it up again. It's water under the bridge."

"Does that apply to us?" He cocks his head to examine me more closely.

"It does if you want it to. As far as I'm concerned, you apologized and took your spanking for those things. I refuse to hold them over your head."

"Oh." He looks thoughtful, standing still, which is a rarity with him.

"Do you forgive me, Monty?" I prompt after a moment.

"Um, yes?" He bites his lip, like he isn't sure he means it.

"You don't have to, you're allowed to be hurt."

One of his mischievous grins tugs at his lips. "I like when you hurt me, Daddy. But yeah, I forgive you."

"Good, come here?" I open my arms up to him and he steps into the offered hug, solid and warm in my arms.

"Thank you, Daddy."

"What for?"

"Agreeing to play with me again. I really enjoyed our scene at littles night."

"I enjoyed it too, Monty."

He lets me give him another squeeze, then eels out of my arms. "So, are you going to tie me up now?" His earlier enthusiasm returns, full force. I relax at having smoothed over his hurt feelings. That's not the type of pain he enjoys.

"Soon. First, I want to go over everything with you. With Angel, we discussed doing a chest harness. Something that's more about the artistic details and less about the bondage. But I know you like to be spanked, so for you, if you'd prefer a tie that would be ideal for that, we can go with something simple instead. Like bending you over a chair and tying your limbs to the chair legs. Or we can stick with the artsy show in front of the crowd. It's up to you."

"Whatever you had planned for the demo is fine, Daddy." Monty ducks his head.

"We haven't talked about your limits and what you need in any depth. Is there anything I should know? Any health concerns?"

"No health conditions, other than the occasional headache and seasonal allergies. And ADHD, but that shouldn't affect what we do much. I've got techniques and meds that help me. Anyway, it shouldn't be an issue for the occasional scene. When it comes to what we've talked about doing together, bondage and discipline, I've yet to encounter anything I don't like. And if it gets too intense, I have my safewords. I enjoy public sex, but you said that's a limit for you, so going to a private play space for that is fine with me."

"Except being denigrated, that seemed like a limit for you." I can read between the lines that disclosing his ADHD is a big deal for him. From his wording, I get the idea that it's already presented challenges for him in the past.

I know plenty of daddies who have strict rules for their littles to follow and I can see Monty struggling with that, depending on how they structured their expectations. He might be willfully disobedient at times, but I'm beginning to think that choosing not to obey is a way to preempt discovering his best efforts have fallen short of perfection. If he mouths off or breaks a rule, then he has control of the situation instead of leaving himself vulnerable to being found lacking. Or I'm reading too much into his psyche from our limited interactions.

"Yeah. Guess I'm not really into that." Monty shrugs.

"And you enjoy pushing your daddy's buttons." I smile, hoping to ease some of his tension.

"Can't seem to help myself. I'm not always great with impulse control." He returns a shy little smile, still not quite back to his bubbly self under the smiling facade, but I'll take what I can get.

"Okay. Thank you for sharing with me, Monty."

"Thanks for asking, Daddy," he replies with a cheeky grin.

My phone beeps with a five-minute reminder we're on soon. I need to get ready and set up all my gear on the elevated platform that serves as a stage in the public play room. "You ready to get out there?" I check as I pull off the shirt I had on over my harness. I prefer to work with minimal clothing impeding my movements while I'm tying. And Monty's gaze on my exposed torso is a nice perk. He licks his lips hungrily.

"Yes, Daddy."

"Good, you can carry my bag." I gesture to the bag in question, to be sure he knows which one it is. Before he moves to obey, I turn on my heel and head out of the locker room. I intend for the gesture to show Monty I fully expect him to follow with what we need for the demo. From the sounds of him scrambling to catch up with me, he takes that trust to heart.

CHAPTER 5

Monty

Our entire conversation in the locker room is surreal. Most of the people I play with think they know me. I've been a fixture at the club since I was old enough to join. I've played with just about everyone. Or at least, everyone who is open to screwing a pudgy brat of a sub with a reputation for disobedience.

I get that I brought my reputation down on myself. Still stings a bit for it to stick with me over the years and make it impossible to find someone for longer than a scene or two. Martin has always been good about agreeing to spank me when the club isn't too busy and he has time. Which was why I was asking him if he had time for me tonight.

At first, I didn't notice that Martin was wearing the DM arm band. I'd hoped that letting someone else paddle my ass would drive away the desperate hunger for another night with Daddy Luke. Naively, I'd hoped that proving I could get my needs met elsewhere would hold my desire for Daddy Luke at bay. Make it seem less all-consuming.

I realize he isn't *my* daddy. Not the one I fantasize about, but I also can't make myself call him anything else. Not even in my head. Maybe especially not there.

It was weird that he noticed how much it stung for him to dismiss me because of my reputation at the club. And weirder for him to apologize for it. It's far more common for me to be the one apologizing, since I frequently put my foot in my mouth. Or do shit I shouldn't. Like biting his finger the other night. I still feel bad about that, even if he says all is forgiven.

I can't say why I blurted out that I have ADHD. It's not something I share unless I have to. Too many people find out and then that's all they see. Just a diagnosis and all the stereotypes that come along with it. They don't see how I've worked hard to fit into a world designed for neurotypicals and that this is my leisure time. The space where I don't have to mold myself to society's expectations of how people are supposed to behave and think. Except the longer I spend at the club, the more I realize it's still people and they still have expectations I can't always meet.

I want so badly for Daddy Luke to be different. To trust me and want me. When he leaves without watching to see if I'll do as he asked, I take a second to realize he means it as a show of support. Trust. I am not about to let him down, so I heft his bag up and jog after him so we can start the demo on time.

Once we're on the stage, I'm excited to start. Except it's still a demo, so Daddy narrates everything he's doing. Not quite as bad as it would be for a workshop where he is actually teaching everyone in attendance, but trying to pay attention to his descriptions is impossible. I just can't make my mind slow down enough to follow along when he talks about basic safety stuff I've known for ages. Duh, he has something to cut the ropes if I get in trouble. He always does when I watch him playing.

I'd hoped that once Daddy Luke actually gets started tying the harness, I could settle into the scene. Except he's going so slowly and checking in with me so often to demonstrate safe versus unsafe technique that I can't lose myself in the ropes.

My brain flits from him talking about not pinching the nerves in my wrists to Vulcan nerve pinches, then off on tangents about the show I've been buddy watching with Tate. Then I ping back to that one pressure point in my hand that makes my headaches hurt less. From there, I get caught up in trying to recall how many bones are in the human hand. When I can't remember, I shift around to feel each of them moving so I can attempt to count them all.

My fidgeting gets me a gentle reprimand from Daddy. I try to hold still. He smiles and pats my shoulder. His gentle praise grounds me for a minute. That tender smile, directed at me, is like sipping warm honey when I've got a cold, sweet and soothing. But before I know it, I'm fixated on Daddy's promise to take me home and make me fly.

Suspension is something I've wanted to try for ages. I've played with a dom who fucked me in a sex swing once, and that was good, but it's not the same as watching Daddy with his ropes. It would be amazing if I could just sink into the bondage demo, or failing that, fantasies of what I want to do with Daddy Luke. Too bad that isn't how tonight goes. Daddy gives my ear a gentle tug.

"How are your wrists, my naughty boy?"

"Fine, Daddy." I wiggle my fingers just to show him I can. He gives me a smile, then goes back to explaining the ties he's using to knot a pretty interlocking diamond pattern over my pecs. That has me going off on a tangent again.

From diamonds, to snakes, to snakebite piercings, to whether Connor is here tonight since he's got pierced nipples and I wanted to ask him something about our game. When Daddy swats my ass to get my attention, I realize I wasn't doing a great job of holding my position. My fidgeting is making it harder for him to work on me.

Damn it. I wanted to be good for him tonight. Should have taken a lunchtime dose of my meds. I need it sometimes, if I have to focus later in the day, once the morning dose wears off, but then I struggle with falling asleep. It's a balancing act between concentrating on Daddy's instructions and spending the entire evening wired, or needing a bedtime med to help me sleep. Those always make me groggy the next day. I hate spending my weekends with a sleep med hangover. I hold still and try to focus.

Daddy tugs the ropes around my chest until they sit nice and snug. Mm. I like that. Can't wait to have his ropes holding me up in the air. I want it so bad and I hope to hell my shitty performance tonight doesn't make him rethink his offer. It would suck if I screwed that up for myself, since having someone give a flying fuck is totally on my top ten list. Somewhere near the top, if I actually bothered to number them that closely.

I'm so up in my head that it's a surprise when the demo ends and Daddy ushers me off the makeshift raised platform that serves as a stage. He left the harness on me, which is cool. Now that it's all in place, I appreciate the gentle restraint of it hugging my body. The ropes tether my arms behind me to better show off the work. My shoulders are getting sore from the strain, though. I wonder if he'll leave me tied up for my spanking.

Daddy Luke snaps his fingers, drawing my attention back to him again. "Is everything alright, boy? You seem distracted."

"Sorry," I shrug it off as best I can in the harness.

"Do you want me to untie you?" He tugs on the ropes binding my wrists like he expects me to agree.

"If I say yes, do I still get my spanking?"

"Yes, you still get your spanking."

"Then, yeah. Please, Daddy. It's kind of uncomfortable with my arms behind me."

"Not a problem." Daddy Luke sets to work untying me. Without taking it slow for the audience, his movements are quick and efficient, totally assured of his own skill, which is hot. I love having his nimble fingers roving over my body. Even if he isn't really touching me so much as the ropes. It's still nice.

When he's done, he loops the rope into tidy coils. He turns to pack it back into his toy bag. The sight of his back turned to me fills my chest with a hollow ache. I don't want our time together to be over yet.

"Can I carry that for you, Daddy?" I offer, as a way to keep him with me, even though he already said he'd keep playing for a while longer. Anything to keep him close.

"Daddy's got it, sweet boy, let's go put the toys away and then you can have your reward." Daddy Luke shoulders his bag, then lifts an arm toward me in invitation. I go to him without hesitation, letting him loop his arm around my shoulders and draw me away from the stage. His attention fills me with that same warm honey sensation from earlier. Something irresistible and sweet that I can't get my fill of when it comes to him.

CHAPTER 6

Luke

This past week, the sign-ups for my ropes workshop filled up fast. To where I've got a waiting list going now. Tying people up and teaching them to tie up their partners safely are a sideline, not my primary job. My major income is from working with Tate.

We took over his uncle's plumbing business when the man retired a few years ago. Tate's trained as a plumber, so he handles the actual service calls and I handle the business end of things that he hates dealing with. Side hustle or not, the level of interest in the workshop I'm offering is validating.

I'll have to open up more sessions if I keep getting calls from people interested in attending. I'm not sure if it's the demo I did with Monty last week attracting more interest, or something else. That demo was not what I expected. Objectively, it wasn't bad. Monty looks wonderful, bound and at my mercy. But he was acting strange.

I've never seen Monty so distracted while he was playing. His usual behavior is almost hyper-focused on whatever his dom asks of him or else he falls into playful banter. But while we were on the stage, he kept fidgeting and acting like he was a million kilometers away. And not in a subspace sort of way, either. More like daydreaming.

Even afterward, when I had him turned over my knee for his spanking, he kept squirming. I almost stopped the scene before we really got going because something was off with him, except he had his safewords, and wasn't using them. Quite the contrary. He kept his mouth shut and gripped my ankle like a lifeline.

Monty only sank into his usual engagement with his play partner and letting me hear him moan once I'd given him the first several spanks. Then he finally seemed present in the moment. Whining for more and lifting his perfect squishable ass up into each smack of my palm on his bare flesh. From there, the rest of our evening went more like I'd expected. I catch myself fantasizing about fucking his perfect ass far too often lately. Monty is a great lay, but he's more than that too.

My personal cell phone rings with the tone I use for my kinky contacts as I'm finishing up invoicing for the business. I answer. Perks of working from home: I can take these calls any time. Probably another potential workshop sign-up.

"Hello?"

"Hi, Daddy Luke," Monty says. Huh. The boy isn't in the habit of calling me. But he did ask to try suspension. He must want to schedule a private session. I won't say no to that. Though, I probably should, before this goes much further. I need to get it through my head that screwing around with Tate's best friend is off limits. I do not need my dick to make things awkward between me and my brother and business partner. Again. "Have you heard about Adventures?" Monty asks.

"What about it?" I shift the phone to my other ear, apprehension gripping me that something might be wrong with my new club. I'm just getting into the groove there. Surely there isn't a serious issue?

"I guess a pipe burst and Martin has to close the public areas until he can do repairs. The private rooms are still available by appointment, for now."

"I see." What I don't see is why Monty is calling me about this development. And why Martin didn't call Tate. Surely Tate would have told me if he was making an emergency call at Adventures. Then again, he did text me a message about an after hours service call last night. As per our arrangement, he's attached the recording of his detailed verbal report to an unread message in my inbox. I pull up the email on my computer as Monty continues to talk.

"So. They aren't having little nights until they reopen."

"I see." So I won't be getting a repeat of Friday night with him this week. Not that I was planning to attend little night this week. That is Tate's safe space. Considering that we work together, it's just simpler to keep some separation in our sex lives. In the years since our moms got married, he really has become my brother, and I don't want to cross lines with him. Like, by say, becoming fuck buddies with his best friend. I rub my temples.

"And I was really looking forward to playing tomorrow night. You and Quent and Kylee are the only people I'm on good enough terms with to ask about private play areas we might use to meet instead." Monty continues to ramble.

Ah, now I really do see. The boy wants a place to meet up and get kinky.

"Did Kylee say no?" I ask, assuming he already checked with his friends.

"No, not at all. She said Quent could invite us over to play more often while the club is closed. They host sometimes, anyway. But they are selective about who comes into their home, which is fair. I'd just rather play with you again."

"What?"

"I wanted to play with you, Daddy Luke. We don't have to go to

Quent's, since Tate will be there and I get that it's weird for you to watch him or whatever."

"Monty, I'm flattered." I need to let the boy down gentle, but there's no way I can pursue something long-term with Tate's best friend. And we've played together enough in the past few weeks that to go on this way would definitely be leading Monty on. No, best to nip his interest in the bud.

"Yeah." Monty's voice is flat and tight, probably with suppressed tears. Damn it, out of all the ways I could make him cry, this ranks among the worst. "I get it. Um. Thanks for giving me a chance, Luke. Guess I'll see you around once Martin gets Adventures open again."

"Monty, wait." I don't know what makes me say it. The part that can't stand to see a boy miserable in an unintended way, I suppose. "I promised you a ropes session, right?"

"You don't have to stick to that promise." Monty sniffles, the sounds muffled like he's doing his best to hide it. "I get that I screwed up on the stage, I'm sorry, Da-Luke."

"You didn't screw up anything, Monty. You were a wonderful boy for me on Friday."

"But you still don't want to scene with me again." The words are accusing, but his tone is forlorn. I want to comfort him, after how open he was with me last Friday. I don't want to be another person who makes him feel disposable. Good for a quick session and nothing more. Hurting him is exactly the sort of wedge I don't need in my relationship with Tate. And that's on top of genuinely not wanting to hurt Monty. At least, not in ways he doesn't want to be hurt.

"It's not that I don't enjoy playing with you. It's about Tate."

"Tate? Why?" Monty asks, baffled.

"You're his best friend." As if I need to remind him of that fact.

"Yeah, so?"

"So, if we got serious, what do you think that would look like? You two enjoy playing together."

"We do, but it's not sexual between us. We've shared a daddy a few times, but at the risk of TMI, Tate doesn't like sexy play when he's in his little headspace. So even if I'm being your full-time naughty little slut, if Tate comes over for a playdate, he'd sooner color or run around outside than screw."

"Is that information he'd want you sharing with me, boy?" I can't keep the reprimand out of my voice.

Monty's answer is flippant. "He does it at Adventures, in front of the entire club. Pretty much all the bigs there know Tate doesn't do dirty play. You could be one of them, if you wanted."

"It's awkward."

"Why? I guess I don't get it. Only child here, but Tate and the other littles at Adventures are the closest people to siblings in my life and we play together all the time."

"It's awkward, Monty. Did Tate ever tell you how we met?"

"At summer camp. You offered him a hummer in the bathroom after hours." Monty replies, like the story is just a fun fact and not the source of far too much family drama. Talk about adding extra tension to the whole 'blending families' process. We even shared a room for a while, which, let's just say our fling ending at summer camp didn't make my dick stop noticing the hot guy sleeping in my bedroom.

When our moms caught on that there was sexual tension between us, it was awkward as fuck. It would be one thing if we'd been in love, but it really was just sex for both of us. I've never loved Tate as anything but a brother, but I can't be sure of how he'll react to me going after a relationship with his friend.

"Yeah. We fooled around for most of the summer, only to get home and have my mom introduce his mom as her girlfriend. Turns out they'd been together all summer, too."

"Guess you and your mom have similar taste," Monty quips.

I snort, my moms' sex life isn't particularly something I want to dwell on. "The point is that Tate and I don't cross those lines anymore. And it took years for us to work out who we are to each other now. I don't want to let a relationship come between us."

"It's just a few scenes, Daddy. If it makes you more comfortable, we don't have to tell Tate. I understand you aren't offering me a full-time thing, just a few sessions with the ropes and maybe some other light play while the club is closed. Scratch an itch for us both."

"Are you certain that's all you want, Monty?" I ask, because I've seen the way the boy pines for a full-time daddy. And I'm familiar with how fast feelings can grow when you bare your soul to another person by sharing your kinks. The level of intimacy he's already shared with me is a heady thing. It's easy to fall for someone when they are completely vulnerable with you, like Monty is when we're together. Am I really considering this?

"Yes, Daddy. I just want someone to play with for the summer. We don't even have to fuck, if that's the part that's bothering you."

I should tell him no. Encourage him to enjoy playing with his friends at Kylee's play parties for the summer instead of this. "I have a few hours on Friday for the suspension session I promised you. Why don't we see how that goes and decide on more from there?"

"What time should I be there, Daddy?" Monty sounds so eager. I can practically see him bouncing and excited. The mental image of him smiling and happy makes me smile, too. We hash out the details, then I hang up and get back to work. If I'm going to risk driving a wedge between Tate and me personally, then I damn well better stay on top of our professional ties.

It's not just that Tate dislikes the paperwork associated with running the business, his dyslexia makes it difficult for him. More efficient for me to handle this side of things. Tate can read and write. It's just easier, not to mention less stressful, to find workarounds. Like dictating service reports and having me write up and deliver our invoices.

Sure enough, the email he sent me is a voice recording summarizing a service call for Adventures with a note that Martin gets a friends and family discount. Even so, it's a hefty bill to come out after hours and handle a burst pipe. It might be awhile before the club can open again, judging from what Tate's report says. Maybe I should be glad Monty is offering me a way to get kinky in the interim. Right or wrong, I'm looking forward to seeing the boy.

CHAPTER 7

Monty

I spend most of the week looking forward to my session with Daddy Luke on Friday night. I try to convince myself it's only the idea of suspension that I'm so into. But the truth is, I'd be just as happy to see him, regardless of our plans. Still, getting to see him and do something new that I've always been interested in is a definite bonus.

I'm heading across the Lion's Gate Bridge to his place on the North Shore when Tate calls me. Tate is the one friend who I don't mind calling instead of texting, since it's easier for him. His phone does text-to-speak, but he prefers voice chat.

"Hey, Tater Tot," I greet him, unable to suppress my good mood. He doesn't need to know why I'm looking forward to tonight.

"Someone is in a chipper mood," Tate says, giving me a chance to divulge why. With our favorite play space out of commission for the foreseeable future, I get why my bubbly mood might seem strange.

"Um, yeah. It's sunny and nice out. Might go to the beach this weekend. If the weather holds."

"Any reason you can't go tonight?" Tate knows me too well. If it weren't for my plans with his brother, that's exactly where I'd be heading after work on a sunny day like today.

"Busy." It's not even a lie. But the lack of detail isn't like me.

"Mhm." Tate sounds suspicious of my evasiveness, but I told Luke I'd be discreet about meeting up with him. So I'm not going to trumpet the news to the last person he wants involved in our little fling.

"Anyway, what's up with you? Are you calling to chat or did you need something?" I deflect.

"Quent called about this weekend's game. We're postponing for a couple of weeks because Harry has to work this weekend to deal with a screwup with a subcontractor. And when we reschedule, we're playing at his place since the club is closed."

"Okay, cool. Can Q text the address or are you giving me a ride?" If we were chatting in person, I'd play up making that last bit super suggestive to get a laugh out of him. But I'm on the bus, so I'm trying to behave.

"I can pick you up. Quent asked me to let you know about the change in venue. Also, Q wants you to bring more of that fresh jerky you got last time."

"I can do that. The place I get it is near my apartment. I'll swing by after work the night before and grab a few bags. Spicy, original, or curry? Oh, and beef, right?"

"Yeah, beef. Connor doesn't do pork. Why not do a bit of each flavor?" Tate suggests. "It went pretty fast last month."

"Cool. I can do that. Anything else I should bring?" I tap my fingers on my thigh.

"Just yourself and your dice."

"Sounds good. How's your week going? Other than the obvious."

"The obvious being what happened at Adventures with the

busted pipe?" Tate asks dryly.

"Yeah."

"Not bad. Business is steady. It might even be nice to have some extra play parties at Ms. Kylee and Quent's place. Mix things up with a different pool of potential play partners, right?" he muses.

"Yeah. Sure. Um, are you bringing cookies to game night?"

"Do you want me to bring cookies?"

"Yes, please."

"I'll see what I can do." Tate promises. Score. "Guess I should let you go do whatever has you too busy for the beach. I need to give Luke a call to check in about next week's schedule." Mention of his brother nearly makes me choke.

Fuck, does he know? Of course he can't. But it takes an effort to play it cool. "You do that. Call Luke. And stuff. Got to go get busy." I wince because 'getting busy' is exactly what I want to be doing with Daddy Luke. And Tate is probably the last person I should say that to right now. "See you later, bye!"

I hang up. Not at all suspicious behavior. Nope. Nothing to see here. The person beside me stands to get off the bus, which is when I realize we passed the stop closest to Luke's while Tate's call distracted me.

I stand too, and hop off the bus with my seat partner. My lack of attention only translates to having to backtrack a couple of blocks by foot. Hopefully, the extra distance will give Tate plenty of time to talk to Luke and get off the phone before I arrive for my session. At least, that's the silver lining I cling to as I trudge toward Daddy Luke's place. Keeping things from Tate might be harder than I bargained for. Not that there is really anything to hide.

I've scened with plenty of people Tate had a history with. And vice versa. The community is too small for us to completely write off a potential partner solely because they also played with a friend. I mean, unless the friend brought up a safety concern. Adventures is diligent about vetting members, though. So we have more issues with interpersonal drama than reckless play or flaunting consent. Martin insists on making everything that happens in his club as safe as possible while respecting our autonomy.

I really hope the water damage doesn't result in the club closing for good. It would leave a void that's hard to fill in my social life.

I've only been to Daddy Luke's a handful of times before. It's recognizable. An old house with a garage where he keeps his kink gear. It's one of the few in the neighborhood that hasn't gotten bulldozed and renovated into a mini mansion. Tate mentioned it belonged to an uncle on his mom's side who sold it to Luke cheap when he retired and moved East to live closer to his daughter.

I've seen Daddy Luke use his rigging frame on other people. The entire array is set up over a thick padded gymnastics mat and looks solid. This will be my first time going up in the air. I trust him, but there is still a nervous flutter in my chest as I approach the door to knock.

When he answers in nothing but a low-slung pair of lounge pants, he's on the phone. Damn, he's hot. I want to lick that broad, furry chest. Bury my face in his pits and breathe him in while I dry hump him. Daddy Luke smiles and waves at me through the storm door, but he holds a finger to his lips in a silent request for me not to talk yet. So, that's probably Tate on the line.

I nod, disappointment twists in my gut at being kept a secret, but I just stand and stare at his landscaping. The outdoors kind, not his chest hair. As though it doesn't bother me at all to stand here cooling my heels. The flowers are hitting their peak bloom. Tulips, I think. Guess that's another sign that spring is turning into summer and more beautiful beach weather is on the horizon. The storm door creaks open.

"Hey, sorry about that. Tate called, but I'm all yours for the rest of the evening. Come on in, Monty." Daddy Luke breaks into my reverie.

"Yes, Daddy." I shove down my hurt feelings, eyes downcast, as I step inside his home. He keeps it neat enough, from what little I can see. I'm not here for a grand tour or anything. We go from the mudroom through a door into his garage playroom without pause.

He's got loads of fun stuff we could play with stored out here. But my eyes lock onto the sturdy suspension frame with its hardpoints and the hanks of neatly coiled rope ready and waiting for us. I'm really doing this.

I can stand to keep my mouth shut about him hiding me from Tate if it means I get to soar. Right? Right.

Luke's gaze rakes over me, appraising. I resist the urge to cover up and avoid his scrutiny. I'm not ashamed of how I look, but I am insecure after he hid my presence from his brother.

"Good, I see you wore what I suggested," Daddy Luke comments.

Ah, right, he's not checking me out, just making sure I'm compliant. This might be my first time trying suspension, but it's not my first brush with ropes. I wore a snug tee and a pair of yoga shorts. Good thing I'm not particularly body conscious. The tight clothes don't hide much. "If you wanted, I could strip. To be certain that nothing gets in the way." I wink at him to show I'm not serious, even though I'd love nothing more than to get naked with him again.

"What you're wearing should be fine." Luke dismisses my offer. Ouch, that shouldn't sting. This isn't about sex, it's about getting to try something new with someone I trust implicitly to know what he's doing. "So, for today we're going to do a simple suspension, to get you used to how this all works. I need you to talk to me if anything hurts, tingles, or goes numb. If that happens, we need to adjust to avoid nerve damage. My setup is rated to lift you safely. But it's your life on the line, so you are welcome to take a look at everything and be sure you're happy with it."

"You're the expert." I shrug off his offer. "I trust you, Daddy."

Luke's expression softens at the title. He starts to lift a hand, then clenches it at his side, like he thought better of reaching out to touch me. Well, at least I'm not the only one interested in something more than a scene. Even if he isn't willing to act on it.

His next words make all my warm fuzzies evaporate. "It's still a good idea for you to check. I can show you what to look out for if you play with someone else. This sort of play has risks, Monty. I will do absolutely everything in my power to keep you safe, but you could fall, break bones, sustain nerve damage or even die if something goes wrong."

Is it sad that the part of that statement that really makes me go cold is the mention of doing this with someone else? I'm well aware of the risks involved.

"I get it. RACK, you're obligated to tell me all of that as a responsible dom." Risk Aware Consensual Kink is my jam and I know Daddy Luke knows what he's doing. He's trained with the best riggers in the city for years and I trust him with my life. Literally, in this case. He wouldn't suspend me if he didn't think it was as safe as possible. He's still watching me expectantly, so I go on. "I'm happy to learn whatever you think I should know. But I'm certain I want to do this with you, Daddy. And you know it's not my first rodeo with ropes."

"Sure." Luke raises a brow at me. "But I seem to recall a very distracted boy the last time we played. I need to know you'll be aware enough to tell me if something is off tonight. Understand?"

"I understand. I, uh, took my meds. At lunch. If I need to focus on shit in the evening, I usually need a second dose. But it messes with my sleep schedule, so I try to avoid it and I wasn't planning on playing last week. At least, nothing more than a spanking as part of a hookup. But, tonight I'm good. I can concentrate better, so my mind won't wander off the way it did last time."

"Thanks for telling me, Monty. I'm glad it won't be an issue. Is there anything else I should know about your meds or any conditions? Any other meds?"

"No. Only the ADHD. And like I said, I've got a medication regimen that mostly helps me do the things I need to do with work and stuff. Or you know, focus on what you're doing with the ropes."

"That's good. And I'm used to my bottom drifting off into subspace when we play. But for this I need to know you and your body well enough to avoid any trouble if you are less than present with me, understand?"

"Yep. And I ate a light meal and hydrated before I came over, like you suggested. Even cleaned out, just in case." I give him a flirty wink. "I'm good, promise. Can we get started?" I bounce on my toes and flash him a cheeky grin.

Daddy Luke ruffles my hair and I revel in the affectionate, all too brief, touch.

"Ah, that brings us to my next point. What do you expect once I've got you dangling at my mercy?"

"The suspension is the extent of what you promised, so I don't want to overstep by expecting more than that. But I'd love to get fucked while I'm up there. If you're into that."

"I'm more than happy to fuck your ass for you, Monty. I've got condoms and lube."

"Cool. I'm negative and I get tested regularly. And I'm on PrEP, just, you know, in case it matters. But condoms are good. I love the idea of being bound and helpless while you plow into me. A little latex won't make much of a difference to me."

"Good to know. I'm also on PrEP. But it's going to be a latex-free condom. Allergic to latex, ask me how I figured that out."

"I'm guessing the worst way possible?" I wince. "Did your dick swell up in a not so good way?"

"Yeah. Got a horrid looking itchy rash. The incident happened with Tate at summer camp. We'd been screwing around with oral sex without protection because neither of us had been with anyone else and we were reckless teenagers. But the camp made condoms discretely available, and he grabbed a few, so we decided to try anal our last weekend at camp. Figured the condoms would make it less messy."

"Talk about an interesting first time. You're like the poster child for sex getting better with practice." I tease, already seeing where the story is going. Poor Luke.

"Yeah. It was, um, not our best night ever. It's still a tossup whether I'm glad he volunteered to bottom first. I feel like a swollen, inflamed ass while getting fucked might have put me off bottoming entirely. But at the time, I was afraid my dick might actually fall off or something. Have I mentioned it was not fun?" Luke flashes me a rueful smile that makes me want to kiss him.

"You did. What happened?" I gesture for him to continue. Tate was holding out on me with this story. He's not the sort to be shy about sharing his sexual history among friends. I mean, we fuck in front of each other at play parties. I've screwed around with most of my friends. So our friendship sort of circumvents lots of societal norms. It's odd I've never heard this before.

"Well, we did the deed. It was sort of itchy and uncomfortable at first. But I'd heard enough guys at school complain about how uncomfortable condoms are that I figured it must be normal. Then I got inside him and it felt too good to worry about a minor discomfort. It was my first time, so I didn't know what to expect. It didn't exactly last long, even with the burning and itching. Might not help that I don't mind a little pain with my sex, anyway." He runs a hand through his hair, chuckling self-consciously at admitting to a preference not usually associated with tops.

"Hey, me too." I assure him with a flirty wink. "Nothing wrong with that."

"Right? Some folks don't think a top should enjoy that side of things, though." Luke flashes me a smile.

"Well, those folks aren't worth listening to. Tell me what happened with the condom."

"So, after we finished, I took off the condom and my dick had developed this horrible rash. My fingers got all tingly, too. And we were young and foolish, so we figured it was some sort of instant STI or something. Ended up panicking and getting the camp nurse involved. She took us to an all night urgent care place. Which was mortifying. But yeah, long story short, polyurethane condoms, if that's alright?" Luke ends the story with a self-deprecating chuckle.

"That's why you always bring your own to Adventures, huh? I wondered. It's fine. That's an epically bad first time fail story."

"Yep. Tate was a good sport about it, at least. Pretty sure he was freaking out that he broke my dick, but he took good care of me that night."

"He's a great friend," I agree. Tate's a great guy. But the more I think about it, the more I realize it was probably scary as hell for Tate to seek medical care for his sex partner like that. No wonder he never told me that story. Daddy Luke seems to see the humor in it, though. In the sense of 'gee, I wish I'd realized then that I should consider stopping to investigate why my dick ached as soon as I rolled the condom on'. I like a man who can laugh at himself, even if the events had to be scary and painful at the time of the incident. And I put way more trust in a dom or top who can acknowledge his screwups.

Daddy Luke nods. "A great brother, too. But enough about Tate. Let's get to the fun stuff."

"Yes, please!" I might wriggle my ass a little. I can't help the excitement buzzing through me at getting more play time with Luke.

"Cool. If we're fucking, you can strip before we begin so that I'll have easy access. Only if you're comfortable with that, of course."

"I'm fine with being naked around you. And it's nice and cool in here, without being too cool. Should I take this off now?" I pluck at my shirt.

"Not yet. You can change after we go over what we're both expecting from tonight." Daddy Luke smiles. Before we get started, he walks me through how to inspect all the gear we're using. His suspension frame is a sturdy construct of solid beams. He points out all the features of the hard points he's using, their weight load limits, and why the numbers need to be so much higher than my weight. Apparently, when he lifts me into the air, the ropes will hold up both of us combined, plus forces from any movement. That's stuff I wouldn't have considered, but his knowledge as he explains it only makes me trust him more.

We go over things I should know, questions about what I want and my experience with ropes. What ties are most comfortable for me and which have caused me discomfort in the past.

I love watching him talk about this. His passion shines through, making me long to have even a tenth of it directed at me. But I'll take what I can get. And if that's just one night of earth-shattering sex while I hang from a rope harness, subject to Daddy Luke's whims, then I'm one lucky boy.

CHAPTER 8

Luke

Once I'm sure Monty and I are on the same page and he's ready to play, he strips out of his clothing. The boy is excited. From his fidgeting, I doubt he'll retain half of the safety information I went over with him about how to assess hard points and ropes. That's okay for tonight. I won't let him fall and we'll go over it again until it sticks before I send him off to play with another rigger.

Or I can just be the one who ties him all the time. That would be fine, too. It's not like helping him explore his interest in suspension is the same as a romantic relationship. I've played with dozens of rope bunnies over the years and never had a big falling out with any of them. My previous partners and I have always gone our separate ways when things run their course. Or they find a top who suits them better if we turn out not to be compatible.

Not to say there's no drama. But mostly, things stay civil. Monty might have a mouthy streak, but I can't see him being the sort to cause trouble between my brother and me if we stop scening together. Which, logically, should apply to anything else we do together, too. But I don't date seriously and breaking that streak to get with my brother's bestie sounds like a losing combination.

By that logic, I should have said no to fucking Monty tonight.

But I've been fantasizing about his glorious plump ass since the first time I turned him over my knee and spanked him. There's no way I could make myself turn down the chance to slide inside of him when it is what we both want.

Suspension scenes can be some of the most intense I've ever done, and nothing beats sex with a bottom who is so utterly under my control. Monty is putting himself completely in my hands tonight. His body, his safety, even his life. So I put aside my doubts and worries about what we're doing and focus on the scene as soon as I've got him positioned where I want him. He is standing, knees flexed, under the frame so I can tie his harness in place.

This time, as I wrap the rope around his chest, he sighs and relaxes into my every touch. It's nothing like our demo at the club. Everything is in sync between us. He's relaxed as I wrap my rope around his chest, following the contours of his body. Or at least, he is as calm as I've ever seen the boisterous boy.

I check in with him as we go. Part of the process is learning his body and where to tie my ropes to avoid putting pressure on his nerves. Years of playing with multiple bottoms of all shapes and sizes has shown me that just because I've learned where the nerves typically lie, doesn't mean there's a one size fits all formula for avoiding them. Running my hands over his body to make sure he maintains good sensation adds a layer of sensuality to the scene. Monty moans when I rub over his round belly down to his full hips.

"You like my hands on you, huh, boy?" I observe.

"Yes, Daddy." Monty licks his lips. I trace a finger over them and he nips at me.

"There's my naughty boy." I pinch his cheek. Monty mock pouts. "Up now?" he asks.

"Soon." I push my thumb against his palm in the signal we discussed earlier for him to check in. He squeezes his fist around me. I wrap my fingers around his and he pushes out, spreading his fingers. Good. "How are you doing so far?"

"It's snug."

"Too snug?" I ask, stroking his arms. Monty sighs, like a contented cat at the caress. He really does like to be touched.

"No. It's just right, Daddy."

"Good." My plan is to keep things simple. First, I tie the hanger to the front of the chest harness and secure him to the solid metal ring I'm tying him to, running the suspension line through the ring twice. "I'm going to put a little tension on the line here, don't go up on your toes, alright?" I take up the slack so that he can feel the tension in the line.

"Okay." Monty grins at me as I tighten the rope. It makes the flesh of his pecs stand out beautifully.

"That's it, gorgeous." I praise him as I tie off the line. "How is it now?"

"Good. Bit tighter, still comfy, though."

"Great." I run my hand over his pecs, feeling him up and running my hands over his body to assess his sensation again as he sighs and moans at my touch. "You're so responsive." I praise him. "Now, spread your legs enough for me to run the rope around your thighs."

He shuffles his feet apart. I start tying the hip harness nice and snug around his waist, three wraps around to support his weight, and three wraps around each thigh. It's a simple enough tie and soon he's ready to go up in the air.

"Now?" Monty asks, shuffling his feet.

"So impatient, my naughty boy." I smack his bare ass cheek in a gentle rebuke. "Just need to tie the hanger now." I suit actions to words, looping the rope around the knots on either side of his body. Once I have everything even and secure, I use a climbing carabiner to secure the suspension line. "You ready to go up?"

"Born ready, Daddy." He nods eagerly.

So I hoist him off his feet, stepping between his thighs to guide him into a dangling seated position. Monty moans as his thighs rest against my hips. Then I raise him up enough so that when I step forward, I'll be able to fuck him. Once I have him right where I want him, I tie off the line, securing it with him in the air. "There, you're flying, Monty."

"Oh, this is… Thank you, Daddy."

I step back, letting him soak in the experience of being held off the ground.

He chuckles, tipping his head back. "It's, uh, not as effortless as it looks in the videos."

"Yeah, you have to be fairly fit for some of the more dynamic poses, especially. You alright?"

"I'm good. Wasn't expecting a workout." He chuckles.

"Want me to take your mind off it?"

"Yes, please, Daddy." Monty nods, making his body sway.

I step in to touch him again, positioning myself between his thighs. "Now I can do anything I want to you, boy. I've got you at my mercy." Suiting actions to words, I tease his cock with a gentle brush of my fingers. That makes him wiggle and buck, which makes him swing from the ropes. The fact I positioned myself between his thighs limits how much he can move and keeps anything from slipping out of position.

"Mm. More. Please?" Monty begs. I lean in, like I'm going to suck him, but only blow my hot breath over the sensitive head of his cock as he strains upward ineffectually.

"Ngh. You're an evil Daddy," he whines, panting at the effort of flexing his abs to get leverage he doesn't have in this position.

I've got him right where I want him, his ass at groin level so I can fuck him at my leisure. The mere thought of it has me hard. Monty is hard too. I stroke him again, spitting on the head so my hand glides along his length.

"Daddy! Quit teasing," he keens.

"You don't like that?" I ask, all feigned innocence, as I stroke him again.

"I want you in me," he demands.

"Oh, do you?" I arch a brow at his audacity.

"Yes." He nods again, the motion rocking his ass against me.

"Are you going to ask nicely, like a polite boy?"

"Um, if you haven't noticed, I'm not a polite boy at all." Monty shoots back. "More filthy."

"Hm, should I lower your head down enough to fuck that smart mouth of yours instead? Teach my boy some manners?"

He groans and arches against the ropes. "No, I'll be polite. Please fuck me, Daddy."

"That's a good boy." I give him a firmer stroke as a reward and his eyes flutter shut as he moans, his body sways as I work his shaft. "Tell me exactly what you want, Monty." I release his dick to get out a condom, letting him spin out a fantasy ought to keep him occupied while I do another safety check and suit up to fuck him.

"I want you to stuff your naughty boy full of your cock. Spread my ass and ram it in. Just some lube, no prep. Take me like I'm made for you and you can slide right in and, like, swing me in time to your thrusts. Like I'm a fuck machine, only in reverse."

I bite back a laugh at the last part of his description. The boy really does have a filthy mouth and I have zero objections to what he outlined since we discussed that he'd already prepped before coming here.

I grab the lube and get into position between his thighs. He's at a good angle for this, so I only have to nudge his thighs apart a little more, which puts more strain on him to keep his legs lifted. That's fine, I'm sure I'll hear about it if it's too much for him. I grip his luscious ass. He's damn biteable with the ropes accentuating his curves. That's something to negotiate for another time, though. I angle myself toward his hole, lining up my condom covered dick and pushing steadily inside. Monty bears down as I draw him toward me.

Fucking while I've got my partner suspended never gets old. The thrill of giving Monty something so intense buoys me along toward my climax. The rush of having such complete control blends with the physical sensations of my cock buried in his warm, pliant body and it's the most exquisite euphoria. Monty moans, throaty and low.

"So, good, Daddy."

"You are," I agree, pushing further into him. I fuck him with hard thrusts, using my grip on the harness to move him along my shaft and really drive in deep. He moans with every unrelenting stroke of his body along my shaft. Fucking him like this is a constant reminder of how much he's under my power. I can drive him onto my shaft with a flex of my fingers, and now he is experiencing how heady ceding that kind of control can be. We both are, and it's glorious. Not just the power he's giving me, but the trust that comes with it.

I hold off on coming for as long as I can, trying to make the experience last for my boy. When I'm too close to last much longer, I move my hand to press behind his balls so I can work his prostate on two fronts. My cock head rams into it with every thrust while my fingers massage him from the front.

Monty thrashes his legs. His calves wrap around me, hooking

against me to anchor himself as cum spurts from his cock and his rhythmic clenching drags me over the edge with him. I come hard, holding onto him to keep from falling over. I have to brace myself to stay upright with his heels digging into the backs of my knees as he fights gravity and the ropes, desperate to secure himself against the swaying weightlessness of the suspension.

We cling to each other, panting as we come down from the high of orgasm. When I'm ready to let go of him, I step back and deal with the condom. I return to wipe his groin with a wet wipe I keep out here for this purpose.

"Ow, cold." He tenses. I keep wiping until the heat of my hand mitigates the cold wetness, and he relaxes again.

"Got to get you cleaned up. What did you think of your first time up?"

"Mm. So hot." Monty mumbles with a loopy grin on his face. The boy is flying high. But he's had enough for one night, his muscles trembling from the effort of holding still in the ropes.

"Very." I agree. "Time to come down."

"Daddy, no. I can take it a little longer."

"Nope. We can play again another time, but for tonight you've had enough."

"Boo." He pouts adorably. If his position didn't have him reclined away from me, I'd kiss the pout off his full lips. But the angle makes that impractical, so I set about lowering him back to the mat. I double check that I've got the correct line, then release the knot and ease his legs down. At first, Monty is shaky standing on his own.

"Whoa, head rush." He weaves and titters like he's drunk. Yeah, he's not really ready to stand unassisted yet. The tension on the chest harness will keep him from toppling over, but I want to get him down on the mat before he can fall.

"Are you doing alright?"

"I'm so good," he insists. "The best."

"Like you're drunk?" I suggest.

"Yeah." Monty nods. "Happy drunk. I didn't though. I wouldn't play impaired, Daddy." He sounds so earnest. Like he could really be my eager-to-please little. It makes me want to smooth his hair or kiss his cheeks.

"I know you wouldn't. You're my good boy." I step in to remove the hip harness while he's upright. Monty sways on his feet as I'm removing the last wrap from around his waist. "I'm going to use the other rope to lower you all the way down, okay?"

"For snuggles?"

"Sure, for snuggles." I agree.

"Okay." Monty gives an exaggerated nod.

I check my lines again, then untie the knot on the suspension line. I lower Monty to the ground with one hand on the rope and the other guiding his body gently to the floor. He's heavy, but not more than I can manage, especially with the pulley to do most of the work. I lower down to sit with him.

Once he's lying flat on the mat, I give him time to find his equilibrium. After a few minutes laying still, he seems less lightheaded. I get him to sit upright so I can remove the chest harness, too. He ends up leaning into me, making the task more difficult. I don't begrudge him the desire for contact. How could I, when I want this intimacy as much as he does?

After I remove the last of the rope, I gather him close and hold him in my arms until he starts to shiver. "Are you cold, baby boy?" The endearment slips out, and I leave it hanging between us. I don't want to draw attention to it by backpedaling. It would only give him the wrong idea. Although at this point, I'm not sure if that would be that I want him or that it was a slip of the tongue.

"Yes, Daddy." Monty snuggles into me.

"Let me get us a blanket." I nudge him away, but he clings to my waist, refusing to budge or let me up. "I'll be right back, promise."

"Okay." Monty's grip on me relaxes.

I grab us both a drink first. Water for me, purple Gatorade I picked up earlier today for Monty. Electrolytes to help with coming down from an intense scene. Then I pull out a fluffy blanket and a couple of soft pillows to make us both more comfortable while he adjusts. It takes some maneuvering to situate us both. I prop myself up on a pillow with him reclining against my chest and the blanket wrapped around us both. He wriggles in close, soaking up my body heat. I murmur sweet nothings into his ear about what a wonderful boy he is and how gorgeously he surrendered to me and the ropes. I press the drink into his hand and he sips it.

"You take good care of me, Daddy. Thank you." Monty mumbles sleepily. And I can't seem to recall why pursuing more with him is such a terrible idea when we're both caught up in the afterglow of a fantastic scene.

I should suggest a move to the playroom couch when the floor gets too uncomfortable. My entire reason for keeping one out there is for aftercare like this. Instead, I guide Monty into my home and have him lie on my mattress so I can rub arnica into his skin where bruises are forming from the ropes. He mumbles a refusal when I offer to help him get dressed, so I leave his clothing neatly stacked where he placed them when he stripped.

So much for my concerns about leading Monty on. I can't think of anything less casual than inviting him into my bed post-orgasm for more snuggles, but I can't seem to resist his allure.

After I apply lotion to his rope marks, Monty still seems too out of it for me to put him on a bus home in good conscience. There is something wonderful about having the naked boy dozy and content in my bed that makes me feel a proprietary pride.

I did that, wore him out and gave him a good time. Monty mentioned having a hard time falling asleep when he takes his afternoon meds, so I don't want to wake him from his dozing state. Instead, I climb under the covers with him and we fall asleep together. Despite my misgivings, the two of us tangled together in my bed feels right.

CHAPTER 9

Monty

Waking up naked in a strange bed with a delicious ache in my ass and elsewhere clues me in that I had an excellent night. Even before my memories of last night filter through the muzzy fog of being awake too soon, confirming that our scene was epic. There's a warm body pressed against me, which makes my dick take notice. This isn't exactly the first time I've found myself in similar circumstances. Usually, if I spend the night, it means there'll be another round before my partner and I part ways.

Except this morning, my partner is Luke. The daddy I've wanted since I first laid eyes on him. The one daddy who is off limits because if I drive him off with my attitude, it might put Tate in the middle of our drama. That isn't fair to anyone. On the other hand, we already fucked last night. What's the harm of another round before I head home? Sex isn't the same as a relationship.

We can have no strings sex. I snort to myself. Well, except the literal kind. What I wouldn't give for more of *those* literal strings in my sex life. I'm more awake now, and yeah, last night there were lots of strings. Or ropes, holding me aloft and at Daddy's mercy.

Yep, my dick remembers how amazing last night was, too. My morning wood isn't going away with such filthy thoughts making it pulse with desire.

Even if it wasn't Luke pressed against me, I'd try not to hump my bedmate while he's still sleeping, but I'm really horny. The memories of last night are only making my dick more interested in the warm, sleepy man I'm pressed up against. He smells so good. I nuzzle into his neck, where the clean smell of his woodsy soap is stronger. I want to lick him. Get my mouth all over him.

Luke grinds back against me. His ass feels nice on my dick. But it also rekindles the burning in my thighs. Right where the ropes cradled me last night. The backs are more sore, probably bruised after taking most of my weight while he fucked me. The hazards of suspension, even if it was too amazing to pay much attention to the discomfort last night. I gasp at the sudden jolt of pain mixing with the way my dick rubs against his ass when he moves.

"Somebody is up and ready to greet the day," Daddy Luke teases me, rolling his hips back to give me another press of his ass against my cock.

"Mhm," I agree, crushing him against my chest to keep my arms occupied instead of reaching for his hips to grind him against me harder. "Morning sex is the best part of waking up."

"Oh, is it?" Luke sounds amused.

"Yes, Daddy."

"Do you want to fuck your daddy, boy?" He rocks into me again, like this is some sort of slow sensual horizontal lap dance.

I cling to him, trying to be a good boy who waits until Daddy tells me what he wants. "Yes, please."

"Pull out your pretty cock, then."

I fumble to do as he says, stroking myself because I need the friction and he didn't say not to. Being obedient is hard. I moan. My touch is so much better by virtue of having him telling me what to do. Plus, the added thrill of getting away with a little something extra that he didn't tell me to do.

"Push Daddy's waistband down and slide your dick between my thighs."

"Lube?" I ask. I'm turned on as hell, but the pre-cum beading at the tip of my dick won't last long if I'm fucking between his legs.

"Daddy's got it, you just do as you're told, my sweet, naughty boy."

"Yes, Daddy." I push his pants down enough to expose the round globes of his ass. Then I slide my dick along his crease, past his hole and into the snug furrow between his legs. He's so warm and tight. I hear the snick of the lube being opened and Daddy's moan as the squelching of a slick hand stroking hard flesh fills the air. Daddy groans as my cock head nudges against his balls when I thrust forward until my hips meet his ass.

"Good boy, stay right there for a minute." Daddy reaches between his legs and I struggle to hold myself still, even though I want nothing more than to fuck into the hot tunnel he's made for my cock. The cool lube his hand slicks along my length makes me yelp and buck into him. Daddy strokes roughly along the underside of my shaft. "Go ahead, Monty, fuck me. Rut your dick against me. Let me take you apart all over again."

So I obey, fucking hard between his thighs, moaning as every stroke brings me closer to completion. He presses his legs together, increasing the delicious friction. Daddy Luke reaches around to grip the back of my thigh, unerringly pressing against where I'm achy from the ropes. His touch lights up my nascent bruises as a reminder that he's in control, even if I'm the one thrusting and fucking and taking my pleasure. I'm doing it because he wants it and that amps up the pleasure until my balls are tight and I need to come.

"Daddy, I'm so close."

"Then come for me." His hand wraps around me, catching my

jizz as I thrust against him, coming with a low groan. "That's it, going to use your cum to jerk myself, boy, watch Daddy now."

I hook my chin over his shoulder to obey, still breathing hard from coming. His hand slides along his length, smearing himself in shiny wetness. And it's hot as fuck to know that he's using my jizz to get himself off, using me like that. Sure, it's a little risky, but we talked about testing and I can't make myself care when it's the hottest thing I've seen in a while, possibly ever. It doesn't take long for his own pearly release to add to the mess. I want to take him in my mouth, lick him clean. Taste our combined spunk on his softening cock until he orders me to stop. I whimper with desire at the thought, my dick twitching valiantly in an effort to go again. Not happening, but it's hot to imagine.

"You like that, boy?" Daddy grunts.

"Yeah. Makes me want to lick you clean, Daddy."

He moans at the idea as he pulls my face up for a kiss. "That's a lovely fantasy."

That's a no. Bad enough that he rubbed my jizz all over his dick. He isn't going to let me eat it up. Not when I'm only his temporary boy. That's the responsible decision. If I was really his boy, though, we could do it. Maybe I can't have it today. But some day, when I find my forever daddy. Hell. If I was really his boy, I could have woken him up with my mouth around his dick instead of prodding his ass with my hard-on.

"Thank you for the scene, Daddy. And letting me stay the night. I guess I should head home now, huh?" I ease my limp dick out from between his thighs so I can roll away from his back. As I swing my legs out of the bed to sit on the edge, I try not to focus on the sounds of Luke adjusting his pants.

"You have plans?" Luke rolls onto his other side to face me, propping his chin on his hand as he watches me.

"No, just going to the beach to soak up the sun." I should get up. Put distance between us instead of lingering in this downright domestic afterglow. It's one thing to fuck during or right after a scene. But what we just did, a leisurely vanilla morning after orgasm, is skirting the lines between a scene partner and something more like friends with benefits.

"Sounds fun. You don't have to rush off if you want to stick around for breakfast. We can be friends, Monty."

I consider his offer. I'm not sure I can be friends with him. Not after the way he blew my mind last night. Not without wanting more. But he's Tate's brother, so running off would probably be rude. "I can stay, if you're sure it's not an imposition. Only for breakfast, though. I want to stake out a perfect spot on the beach. It's my favorite, fun in the sun."

"So, the opposite of Tate?"

I laugh. "Yeah, your brother is not into outdoor activities. The trick is to find things outside where he can let his little side out to play."

"He's always been like that. Tate hated that camp where we met. Took any excuse to hide inside as much as possible."

"Excuses like sucking your dick?" I shoot him a look over my shoulder. Those stories Tate *did* tell me. Like the time he snuck into the equipment room to screw around with Luke. Volunteering for kitchen cleanup so they could linger alone once the other campers and their counselors were at the evening's campfire. Even feigning an injury to get Luke to escort him on a trip to the first aid station when Tate knew the nurse was taking her lunch and the building would be empty.

"Among other things." Luke says nonchalantly. He stands and stretches, his lounge pants barely cover his delectable ass and there is a distinct wet spot at his groin. He grimaces and grabs a new pair from his drawer. The view of him wiping his dick and pulling on fresh pants makes me keenly aware that I'm completely naked.

"Are my clothes still out in your playroom?" I ask as I stand.

Years in the scene have pretty much erased most of my body consciousness. I don't mind being naked in his presence. Early on, I got hung up on having more of a belly and thicker thighs than most of the subs I saw, but I don't have a problem with my size these days. I'm fit enough to do the things I enjoy and I have no shortage of willing partners when I want to play. Part of that is being used to spending time in kinky spaces in front of a crowd in skimpy attire. Or nothing at all if the venue allows, like at a private play party.

Part of it is the body positive culture at Adventures. I've surrounded myself with people who see me as a whole person. And Luke is no exception to that. His eyes track over my body, admiring my curves as I cross the room.

"Right where you left them, yes. You can put them on after we eat." Daddy Luke says it with the authority of a command. I shiver at being treated like I'm his. I've told him this is the sort of thing I want. It's so tempting to let myself imagine I could have this all the time.

But I can't and getting a taste of it might wreck me when it's all over.

If I was a good boy, I'd tell him 'yes, Daddy.' I'd wait to be told what to do. Or maybe ask if he wants me to cook for him. I am not an obedient boy. I ignore him and walk right out of his room, through his kitchen to the mudroom, and try the door to the garage. It's locked. Daddy Luke follows behind me, pulling on a shirt before he leans against the doorframe, arms crossed and a disapproving expression that he has fixed on me.

"Did you not hear me, boy?"

"You said my clothes are where I left them." I tug ineffectually at the door. It doesn't budge.

"What else did I say?" Luke arches a brow at me, making no move to help with the lock.

"That I could have them back after we eat. I want them now. I'm not your boy. You aren't my daddy and we didn't discuss this being a scene. I want my clothes now." I stomp my foot, mad at him and mad at myself for that first slide into little space. Him acting like an authority figure who has a right to call the shots and punish me makes me want to be the boy who pushes his buttons. Fuck. I don't want to be like this. Defiant for the sake of it.

I really *don't* want to get dressed. I want his eyes on me, admiring me. But I need to see what he'll do. How much he wants me.

And part of me is genuinely peeved because we really didn't discuss him being my daddy outside of a scene. He's in the wrong here. Not me.

Luke straightens up and drops the toppy act. He comes to stand beside me and pulls a key out of his pocket to open the lock. "Sorry, my bad, Monty." He pushes the door to the garage open for me. "You asked if I'd be your daddy when we play together. I thought this counted. I should have checked with you before assuming we were on the same page. You can get dressed whenever you want to. There's a package of wipes beside your things if you want to clean up first."

"Oh." I stalk over to the heap of clothing I left in here last night, wipe myself clean, and hastily dress. Luke only follows me as far as the door, giving me space. Space to admit that, yeah I *did* ask him for that. I mostly meant when we were at Adventures. But this morning had been us playing together. Daddy Luke telling his boy how to get off. Sure, it wasn't the kinkiest thing we've ever done, but it still fit the broad definition of what I'd asked him for. "You'd want to be my daddy for this sort of thing?"

"What sort of thing? Everyday tasks like eating breakfast? Yeah, that is part of what you said you wanted, right? A daddy to take care of you and fuss over you?" Luke is still standing in the doorway, watching me tug my snug clothing into place. His eyes rove over me, hungry for more.

"Yeah." I shrug. If I act like it's no big deal to be getting exactly what I want, it might keep me from getting my hopes up about having this long-term.

"So, feeding my sweet naughty boy his breakfast before we go play at the beach falls under that description, right?" Luke arches an eyebrow at me.

"It does." I chew my lip. It fits, but it's also a lot to ask. The trust I've offered him to do an easily defined scene comes with limits. It can't blur into my real life and make me feel things the way this will. If I let him in enough to be his boy for a beach day, it will hurt when it ends. And it will end. Not ten minutes ago, I threw a tantrum because he asked me not to get dressed before breakfast, for fuck's sake. That's a damned simple command, and I rebelled just because he asked it of me.

Or no, I rebelled because I got scared of what it meant. But still. I'm going to scare him off. It's a matter of time. And I shouldn't put us in this position. One thing is for certain, I can't put Tate in the middle of my latest spectacular fuckup in the making.

"Tell me what you're thinking, Monty?" Luke asks.

"I want that." The truth slips from my lips, unbidden.

"You can have it."

I shake my head. "No, because it will all blow up and I don't want to risk my friendship with Tate over a fling."

"Is that what this is? A summer fling?" Luke asks. It sounds like a genuine question, no judgment. That makes it easier to answer than if he was challenging me to call it something else.

"Maybe? While Adventures is closed. It would give us both a

way to play regularly over the summer."

"Okay. Well, how about this? We play as much as we like over the summer and we keep Tate out of it. That way, he never has to choose sides because he isn't part of it at all. Then, when Adventures reopens, we can discuss what happens next."

"So, we'd both keep the fact that I'm your temporary boy from him?" I ask, hating the word temporary in that sentence. But isn't temporary better than nothing?

"If that's what you want, yes."

I chew my lip, considering. Tate will be pissed if I lie to him about this. More than he'd be about me and his brother hooking up. Heck, Tate probably won't care that I'm playing with Luke. He knows about my crush. He *will* care if either of us gets hurt. And I don't want to stress him out worrying about the inevitable heartache when it ends. "That's what I want. No lying to him, though. If he asks, we tell him the truth, but no volunteering information."

"Deal. While we're on the subject of negotiations, why don't we talk more about what we both want and expect out of this arrangement over breakfast?"

"That's probably a good idea."

Luke holds the door open for me, then locks it back up before trailing me into his kitchen. I sit at the kitchen island and watch him rummage in his fridge for eggs, milk, and bacon. "What do you prefer for breakfast? I can make pancakes, if you like?"

"Dinosaur shaped pancakes?" I ask, letting myself slip into the idea of Luke really being my daddy and taking care of me while it lasts.

He turns a sweet smile on me and nods. "If that's what my baby boy wants. Can you tell me what you want from your daddy while I cook?"

I nod. "I want you to take care of me. Like this, feeding me, helping me with stuff like sunscreen, cuddles, playtime, giving me rules and punishing me if I break them."

"Punishments like spankings?"

"Yes, please." I bounce in my seat.

Daddy Luke chuckles as he pulls out a clear plastic squeeze bottle and starts measuring out ingredients. "That might not be the most effective punishment for you, my naughty boy; how about corner time?"

"No, I'd rather have a spank, Daddy." I shake my head, intent on watching him preheat a griddle on the stove and make the pancake batter. He pours the dry ingredients into the narrow container with a funnel.

"And that's exactly why I'm thinking you can have spanks as a reward for good behavior and corner time if you're naughty."

I pout and cross my arms over my chest. "But that's not fun."

"I know, but it might help you learn better manners, don't you think?" He asks me as he pours in the wet ingredients.

"Is that a rule?"

"Yes. I want my boy to be polite. Do you want Daddy to control your orgasms?"

"If you want to." I shrug. I've already told him the most important parts for me. If he wants to show he cares by controlling that part of my life, that's fine by me.

"I do. You only come with permission while you're mine."

"Okay." I love the sound of being his.

"Do you want your dinosaurs colorful?" He offers me a box of food coloring.

"Purple dinosaurs, please." I point at the blue and red.

"See, your manners are improving already," he teases as he adds the colors. Daddy twists the lid onto the bottle.

"Can I shake it up?" I reach for the container, making grabby hands.

"Sure you can." He caps the lid and offers it to me. I shake until the batter is all bubbly, the dry ingredients are mixed in, and the blue and red have swirled together into a brownish purple. I hand it back to Daddy. He uncaps the batter and draws the first batch of dinosaurs on the hot griddle, each one a different species.

"Are we having bacon with the dinosaurs?" I ask. "T-Rex likes to eat meat."

"Sure. Does my boy want some delicious meat in his mouth?" Daddy turns on the oven. He's still watching me out of the corner of his eye.

"Yes, Daddy. I always want your tasty meat in my mouth." I agree, licking my lips lasciviously.

He coughs like he's trying not to laugh. "What would you like to drink?"

"Juice." I reply, trying not to think about his juices on my face after I've had a mouthful of his meat.

He arches a brow at me, like he can follow my filthy line of thought. "Juice, what?"

"Juice, please, Daddy?" I shuffle in my seat.

"Sure. I think I've got orange juice. Do we need to swing by your place after we eat so you can take your meds?"

"Yeah. And my swim trunks."

"Sounds good. Sippy cup?"

"Nope, I'm a big boy."

"Okay." Daddy pours me juice. He also sets two cooling racks in

a cookie sheet and covers them in strips of bacon before popping it into the oven. I sip my juice while he flips the dinosaurs.

"So, you know what I like. What about you? What do you want from this, Daddy?"

"I want to spoil my boy. I enjoy spanking and fucking you, Monty. Other than being a daddy, I'm mostly into my ropes. I can bring pain play into the equation once I've got you in the air. Or not. That's up to you, though you seemed to enjoy the sex last night. And I loved tying you up and having you at my mercy. We can do more of that, if you're into it?"

"Yes, please! Lots more of that. Aerial spanks and sex." I bounce in my seat, wincing as that makes my sore thighs sing. Yep, definitely bruised. "Maybe not right away, though. Guess I'm a little sore. Not used to it." The rest of me is achy, too. It took more muscles than I'd have expected to be tied up and dangled from the bondage frame. If we're doing this, I suppose that's something I'll be getting used to. The thought makes me grin.

Daddy gives me a concerned frown. "I've got more arnica cream if you're bruised, baby boy."

"Will you rub it all over my tender bits?" I tease, giving him a coy look.

"If you want me to." He plates up the first batch of pancakes and sets to work drawing six more dinosaurs with the ease of someone who has had practice. Thinking of him sitting here with another little makes me jealous and I shove those thoughts away. For now, he's mine.

"I do. And after that we'll go to the beach." I declare it like being a demanding brat will erase my insecurities. It doesn't. All it does is drive people away and make me even less confident in my ability to be viewed as boyfriend material.

"Will we?" Daddy asks, arching an amused brow at me. At least he seems to find my antics endearing, so far.

"Yes."

"Yes, what?"

I roll my eyes. "Yes, please, Daddy."

"Good boy. Now, for the really important question."

"Yeah?" I ask, apprehensive.

"What's your favorite dinosaur? Is it a T-Rex?"

"Nope. Maiasaura."

"Oh?"

"Yep. They're from Montana. Like my name … sort of. And they had big herds, and the parents took excellent care of their young."

Daddy watches me talking about dinosaurs and his face gets all soft and caring the more I talk. Like he can see right through me to the heart of my words. That I wish I had a big herd to belong to and a nurturing daddy to look after me. Not that my parents sucked. But after my dad died when I was twelve, Mom mostly went through the motions.

Now I understand better. She could barely keep herself together in her grief, let alone dealing with a budget that just didn't balance without Dad's income. Not to mention making sure I got through school with my issues concentrating compounded by the loss. But at the time I was a grieving kid. It felt like I'd lost both parents when she spent all her time working and could barely function after pulling double shifts while juggling multiple low-paying jobs.

Daddy Luke flips the second batch of pancakes.

"Close-knit families, huh? Just like my Montysaurus and the other littles at Adventures?"

"Yeah." The nickname and the fact he gets what Tate and the others mean to me makes my chest squeeze and my heart go all

fluttery. "Do you have a favorite dinosaur, Daddy?"

"Canada Geese? They let me relive the velociraptor scene from *Jurassic Park* whenever I visit a pond. Or park."

I laugh at that, picturing him being chased by enraged honking geese. Those birds are mean. Not to mention territorial. "Ooh, we should totally do that! Can we? Dinosaur chase scene reenactment, please?"

My enthusiasm makes him chuckle. "We'll see, my naughty boy. It might not be as much fun as you are imagining when you're actually getting pecked to death."

"Worth it to be eaten by a dinosaur. Make sure that's what they put as my cause of death, though, promise?"

"Here lies Monty, who died by dinosaur attack." Daddy Luke sounds all sad and stern while he fakes eulogizing me. He keeps up the solemn act as he pats my hands. "I'll do what I can."

"Good. Can you make me a Maiasaura?"

"Got a picture?"

"Yep." I pull one up on my phone and he traces the outline of my favorite dinosaur with the last of the batter while I watch. The room smells like bacon. As the last batch of dinosaurs cooks, he makes himself coffee. I'm not a fan of drinking it, but I enjoy the smell of it brewing, especially mixed with the mouthwatering bacon. And this whole tableau is so devastatingly domestic it makes me yearn for more. Daddy Luke might just be everything I've ever wanted.

CHAPTER 10

Luke

When we get to the beach, Monty is bouncing in his seat. It takes a few turns around the public parking area to find a spot. Plenty of other people are out enjoying the sunny weather today.

We both grab our bags before exiting the vehicle.

"Can I call you daddy in public?" Monty asks, taking my hand and skipping at my side as we walk along a path through a grassy park area toward the sandy beach.

"If you want." I swing our hands, keeping pace with his excited stride.

"I do. Will you help me with my sunscreen, Daddy? And I can do yours, too."

"Sure, Monty, if that's what my boy wants."

"It is. Look, there's a pond over there with swans and ducks in it. And a playground over there, but the best spot is over here. There are big old logs you can sit on and set up a beach towel and stuff. And most of the people stick closer to the other end."

"Do they?" I ask, amused at his delight in being here, out in the sun. He nods, leading me to the spot he likes. We spread out our towels. Monty pulls off his shirt and hands me his sunscreen, the sweetest plaintive look on his face as he waits for me to slather him in lotion.

As soon as I start, I can see why he wanted this. It's the perfect excuse to smooth my hands over every inch of him as I rub in his sunscreen. It's an intimate act. A gesture of caring, but there is also a sensuality to it. This is something I know he's wanted. I can see it in the way he leans into my touch. The adoring smile on his face as I instruct him to turn so I can get his back.

Monty shivers when I tell him to close his eyes so I can get his face. The vulnerability of his expression when he turns toward me to let me caress the planes of his cheeks just about does me in. This boy is precious, and he's mine. At least for the summer. We are definitely coming back to the beach as often as the weather permits.

I enjoy touching him like this. My boy looks delectable in his trunks, his round tummy on display. It makes me want to lick him, but that's for later. At home. Preferably when I've got him tied to my bed and writhing with pleasure.

Best not to think too much about later, because my swim trunks suck at hiding my erection. Monty notices and winks at me, turning to brush his fingers over my bulge as he takes the bottle of sunscreen from me.

"Does Daddy like what he sees?"

"You know I do, brat."

"Good. My turn to do you now, Daddy." He waggles the bottle at me. Damn, but do I want him to do me, in ways that we absolutely cannot get away with on a crowded public beach.

Monty winks at me, making a show of squirting the lotion into his palms and rubbing it into my skin. He clowns it up, focusing most of his attention on feeling up my pecs and shoulders, and trying to slip his fingers down the back of my trunks. His antics escalate until I have to swat him away and remind him that if he wants his spanks, he has to behave in public.

"Naughty boy, do you want a spanking?" I say, low and menacing.

"Yes, please, Daddy." Monty nods, his hand freezing on my lower back.

"Then behave." I grab his wrist and tug him away from my waistband.

Monty pouts. "I always behave, Daddy. Just sometimes, I behave badly." He gives me an exaggerated wink.

That makes me chuckle. I shake my head at him and try to look stern. "You are incorrigible. I was thinking of strapping you to my bed tonight, but I guess if you'd rather get in trouble..."

"No, I'll be a good boy. Are the hardpoints I saw on your bed frame strong enough to suspend me over the mattress?"

"They are, otherwise what's even the point, right?" I had the bed made custom with that express purpose in mind. Well, not Monty in specific, but I've always enjoyed playing with people of all body types, so I installed hardpoints rated to support bigger bodies like his.

"Awesome. It's like I'm fucking an IRL spiderman who can string me up in his web."

"Boy." I put a warning in my tone, because I'm seriously turned on and he is not helping matters. Monty's gaze flickers to my groin and he laughs.

"I can sit on your lap and make it better?" He suggests hopefully.

"If this wasn't a public beach, I'd let you do a whole lot more than sit on my lap, you naughty boy. As it is, you are getting corner time when we get home. Polite boys do not tease their daddies with public sex."

"Some boys do," he insists.

"*My* boy doesn't. Now, what do you want to do first?"

"Swim." Monty gives a decisive nod and gestures toward the water. "Then dry off in the sun, and after that sand castles."

"Do you want Daddy to watch you swim or join you?"

"Watch me?"

"Sure. Don't go out too far."

"Promise. And if I'm good, I can get a spank tonight, right?"

"Oh, you're getting a spanking tonight, alright." I pull him close and claim a demanding kiss. He opens to me like he craves nothing more than to let me own his mouth. When I pull away, he chases after my lips with his tongue and I press my mouth to his ear. "Because Daddy can't wait to make your perfect tight ass burn red before he buries his dick deep inside of you tonight."

Monty whimpers and leans into me, like he wants nothing more than that exact thing. His hard dick rubs against me as he leans in close.

"Yes, Daddy." he agrees, licking his lips hungrily. "You know, we *could* skip the beach…"

"No." I step back. "Now, go play. Hopefully, the cool water will make your trunks fit a little less snug." I wink at him and he pouts as he turns toward the water, walking a little stiffly to hide his arousal. Turnabout is fair play. And watching him cavort in the waves does nothing to help my own erection, but I can ignore it.

I lounge facedown on my beach towel, dick still uncomfortably hard, but at least out of view. Strategically trapping my erection under me against the hard-packed sand at least dials it back to half-mast, no matter how much I want to get my hands on my boy again. I can wait. He's having so much fun, I'll happily wait all day for him to get his fill of this.

CHAPTER 11

Monty

I might've made an epic fail. It's pretty obvious that I suck at putting sunscreen on a hot guy by the time we're ready to leave the beach. The only part of Daddy's torso that hasn't burned to a bright lobster red is the area over his pecs where I got distracted by touching his muscles. I spared his back and biceps the worst of it, but I guess I neglected to rub the lotion into most of his upper chest, belly, and sides. He just felt so good. I got caught up in having my hands on him.

It's not a great excuse. I could tell how much Daddy loved having his hands on me too, but he actually did a wonderful job taking care of me. I didn't get burnt at all. Long after this fling ends, I'll treasure the memory of how amazing it was to have him turning me, lifting and massaging each limb, tipping up my face with tender care. He rubbed lotion into every bit of my exposed skin, including my folds. He treated every inch of me with such attention to detail. It's exactly what I've always fantasized about finding in a daddy. Someone who cares about and for me.

"I'm so sorry," I apologize again, glancing over at him as we drive back to his place. Daddy puts his hand on my thigh.

"I'm not mad, Monty."

"You sure? I'd be mad at me."

"It's my job to take care of you. That's what we discussed, right?"

"Right." I agree warily.

"So, it is not your job to take care of me. I should have realized where you were touching me, and where you weren't and gone back to touch it up afterward. Or else told you to do a better job. As things stand, since I've got your handprints sunburned onto my pecs. It's only fitting that I return the favor and put my handprints all over your gorgeous ass, right?"

I squirm in anticipation, but I still feel guilty. I shouldn't get a reward for screwing up something so basic. He shouldn't have had to redo his sunscreen after I offered to help him. "I'd really like that, Daddy. But I was naughty."

"Are you asking for corner time?"

"No." I shake my head, then sigh. "No, I don't want corner time, Daddy. But I think I earned it?"

"You earned five minutes for teasing me with sex after I told you to stop. And you're getting your spanking afterward because Daddy wants to give it to you. Unless you object?"

"No. Still kinda guilty, though."

Daddy squeezes my thigh. "If you want to make amends, you can rub aloe into my sunburn after your corner time to help make it better."

"Thank you, Daddy. It won't happen again. I mean, if you even want to go back to the beach after this."

"I do. A little sunburn is a minor inconvenience compared to getting to see my boy so happy and carefree. You are a delight and I'm glad I got to share the day with you, Monty."

"You are? I mean, I thought you might get bored, just sitting there?"

"I wasn't just sitting there. Sometimes watching my boy get to be himself and be happy is my idea of a good time. Besides, I had a podcast to listen to while you were busy. It was very relaxing."

"I'm glad you weren't bored."

"Not in the least. We'll have to go again soon."

It's on the tip of my tongue to suggest we make it a playdate, invite along Quent, Tate, and our other friends. But that would mean telling Tate. And we agreed not to. So the fantasy of playing in the sand with my friends while my indulgent daddy looks on, chatting with the other bigs, will have to remain a fantasy for now. It probably makes me a greedy boy to want more after the nearly perfect day I just had with Daddy Luke. Guess I'm greedy.

When we get to his place, Daddy orders me to strip as soon as we're inside and shows me to the corner where he wants me to stand. He explains the rules to me. No talking or moving or anything. After he explains the rules, he sets a timer and walks away.

I hate every second of being left alone and ignored. It's fucking awful. I don't want to be naughty when this is the result. It's stupid and pathetic, but I lean my face on my hands and cry at how wretched it feels to be left alone like this. Rejected and unwanted and alone.

It's like standing here is a constant gnawing reminder of all my inadequacies. All the ways previous partners told me I didn't measure up. Fun for a scene, but too much work for a proper relationship.

Way to disprove that, when I can't even cope with what might possibly be the mildest punishment a daddy has ever dished out to his boy. Thinking about how pitiful it is to be breaking down over something so innocuous only makes me cry harder. When Daddy comes back to get me, the timer still hasn't beeped, but it seems like it's been an eternity. I stop trying to hide my sniffles at his touch. He's here. He came back. Daddy will make this better.

"You can turn around now. Your corner time is over, Monty." Daddy puts a hand on my shoulder. I must have missed the timer beeping. I was too off in my own world to hear it. Or else why would he be telling me it's over? I fling myself into his arms, sobbing, heedless of his sunburns. He winces at the impact and I pull back, stumbling right into the wall. Utterly miserable, I slide down to sit in the corner.

"I'm sorry. I'll be good from now on. Promise." I can't make myself meet his gaze. I don't want to see him disappointed in me right now.

Daddy crouches down at my level and opens his arms to me again. When I dart a glance at his face, he doesn't seem upset; he looks stricken. I cling to him again. If he doesn't mind the burns, then I'm not denying myself the comfort he's offering me. "Oh, baby, why are you crying?"

"I don't know." I sniffle. My lips tremble, and I can't stop the tears coursing down my cheeks. "I don't know." I repeat. "Don't leave me." I cling to him and he rocks me. "Please. I promise I'll be good, just don't stop wanting me."

"You don't have to be perfect for me to want you, Monty. Corner time isn't about showing you I don't want you, or pushing you away. I think this might be a limit for you? I'm sorry, I should have checked in sooner."

"Sorry." I swipe at my face. "I didn't realize it was going to be so bad until it happened. It seemed like it lasted for hours. I didn't even notice the timer beeping."

"That's because it didn't. I realized something was off with you when you started sobbing. I've got you now. Cry it out, my Montysaurus."

So I do, letting him hold me and make all the terrible thoughts about being unworthy leak away with my tears. Maybe I'm not the best boy out there, but I'm good enough for Daddy Luke to want to hold me. Even when I'm a snot-faced wreck over something most people would consider trivial. He doesn't press me for answers or try to rush me, just holds me close until I've cried myself ragged and my breathing has calmed.

"Better?" he asks.

I nod. "Yeah. Thanks, Daddy."

He kisses my forehead. "Nothing to thank me for. I'm sorry I pushed you too far. Can we talk about what happened?"

I shrug. "I'm not really sure. Guess it seemed like you didn't want me. Like you were banishing me. Or... I don't know. Like you wanted to be done with me? Like, this was a taste of what you'd do if I *really* upset you. That you might send me away entirely if I don't stay in line."

"Okay. Thank you for explaining. If we go our separate ways, it won't be because you're a naughty brat. I knew that going into things. You're rambunctious, impulsive, and silly when you play. That's part of what I like about you. We'll be finding another way to punish you. Corner time obviously makes you insecure and I want my boy to be certain that Daddy will always care for him."

"No more corner time?" I ask.

"No more," he agrees. "Do you want to come snuggle with me for a while before dinner?"

"Can I have my spanking now?"

"Do you still want it?"

"Yes. Spanks and sex, and then dinner. Please." I tack on the polite word as an afterthought. It makes Daddy smile and stroke a hand over my long hair.

"If that's what would make you feel better, then that's what you shall have, my little Montysaurus."

The sweet pet name fills my insides with warm fuzzies. Instead of answering, I grab Daddy's hand and haul him toward the bedroom. His indulgent chuckle tells me he doesn't mind my impatience. The way he holds me while he makes my ass glow with the growing burn of a lengthy spanking tells me he still wants me better than any words could.

Daddy draws my spanking out for a long time. He makes it into foreplay that flows naturally from uncompromising hard swats, to rough caresses, to Daddy parting my cheeks. He slicks me up with lube and dons one of his special condoms to slide inside of me.

I swear it seems more like making love than anything else I've ever experienced. Especially when he curls around me and holds me with his softening cock still as deep inside me as he can get, only pulling out when he's too soft to stay inside. Even then, he doesn't let go of me until his stomach growls, making us both laugh and prompting him to fix us dinner.

CHAPTER 12

Luke

I had no intention of spending the entire weekend tangled together with Monty when I invited him over for a rope session. That doesn't mean I regret the change in plans, though. Not in the least.

If I only get until Adventures reopens to win my boy over to the realization we're a good match, then we need to make the most of the summer. I've got limited time to prove that he's everything I want in a boy and more. So I invited him to stay for the entire weekend.

He fell asleep after I fed him last night, and now he is curled up against me, arms wrapped around me like I'm his favorite stuffy. For all his outbursts and difficulties with following directions, what I see when I look at the man beside me is someone desperate to be loved and accepted for himself. Including the exuberant side of him that lacks impulse control and struggles to focus. I want to be the person who gives him that unconditional care he desires.

Turns out that under the bratty facade, Monty is damn near the perfect boy for me. It's a shame Tate met him first. But really, should that matter? It's not as though Monty and my brother are —or ever were—an item. Is it so wrong to date him just because they're friends?

No. Monty said the problem is that he doesn't want Tate caught in the middle if Monty and my relationship sours. But I've yet to part on bad terms with an ex. It's not so hard to be cordial. Then again, I've never let a relationship progress to where a partner could reasonably hold a grudge about it.

If I like a play partner enough to make seeing them a regular thing, then we play more. Sometimes, even with some degree of exclusivity, and when things run their course, we part ways. It can be that simple with Monty, too. And I have the summer to show him that. If everything goes my way, by the club's grand reopening, Monty will realize how special he is to me, and I'll get him to stick around long-term. If not, I'll always have the memory of him, naked body and soul, as he begs me to fuck him harder. The sting in my hand nothing on the way I know his ass must feel after his spanking.

I idly stroke his back while I lay there next to him, considering what to do with our Sunday. Monty said he didn't have plans. We could play again, maybe with the ropes? His bruises need time to heal before we try another suspension session, but we can still do less intense bondage. Or I could wake my sweet boy with a blow job. He mentioned thinking that wake up sex is hot. That's not the same as saying he wants it with me, though. Another time, when we've discussed it first.

This won't be the last time he wakes up in my bed. I can afford to be patient. We spend a lazy Sunday at home, filling the time with cooking for him, coloring on my back patio, sex, and some light bondage. When Monty crawls laughing out of my bed early on Monday morning, flushed from letting me blow him before he has to rush off for work, I get up with him.

"You don't have to cook for me, Daddy. I can grab something on the way."

I wave off his half-hearted protest. The longing glance he shoots between me and my kitchen belies his words. "I want to take care of my boy. I enjoy feeding you home cooking, Monty."

"If you're sure it's not too much trouble." He shuffles his feet, glancing toward the exit.

"You are no trouble at all." I take his hands and kiss him soundly. Monty stops fidgeting and relaxes against me. I love that, the moment he lets go and gives in to me. It's even better when I've got his beautiful body framed in my ropes, or turned over my lap for a well-earned spanking, or naked in my bed. But I'll take the soft sigh against my lips and the curve of his belly pressing into me as he lets himself relax.

"Plenty of people would disagree with that assessment, Daddy." Monty gives me a coy look, but I still hate hearing that's how he views himself. As too much trouble. Instead of fighting him about it, I kiss him again. I'll just have to show him. I turn him toward the kitchen island where I've got a couple of stools for guests.

"Sit, talk to me about your plans for the week while I cook." I turn to get ingredients for omelets and he takes his seat.

"Nothing major, work mostly. And a play party at Ms. Kylee and Quent's place on Tuesday. Since little night got canceled with Adventures on hiatus. Q has been blowing up my phone asking if I'm bringing anyone."

"Are you?" I ask, hoping the answer is no and glad that the fridge can hide my anxious expression from Monty. He has every right to play with whoever he wants.

"No. Unless you want to come with me?" he asks. I glance back at him, and he's bouncing in his seat. It's on the tip of my tongue to agree as I carry everything I need to the counter by the stove. I preheat the pan, and pull out a cutting board for the green onions, ham, and cheese. Then he scowls. "Except Tate will be there and I don't want it to be a whole thing."

"It's fine. I'll skip the party. Enjoy your night with your friends. But you should have dinner here on Wednesday. And any other night you want this week." I turn to get my coffee brewing while I get my disappointment in check. When I'm ready to face him with a smile, I turn back toward my boy. I crack the eggs into a bowl, whisk them and set aside the bowl while I chop green onions.

"You aren't sick of me already?" Monty asks, with a slight chuckle to make it seem like a joke. I can see through that act easily.

"Not in the slightest. I've got more plans for you, sweet boy. So many plans." I pause from chopping to gesture at the food. "Ham and cheese omelet with onions okay?"

"Yeah. Sounds good. Got any more bell peppers?"

"Sure." I turn to grab one and dice a quarter of it for us. "Anything else?"

"No, that looks good, Daddy. Thank you."

"My pleasure." I pour his eggs into the pan and give them a little stir, then let it cook for a minute while I dig through my junk drawer. This probably isn't the most romantic gesture in the world, but I don't want to beat around the bush. I've found being direct with my desires serves me better. My spare key is buried under some old takeout menus. I pocket it and finish making our omelets. I pour him orange juice before fixing my cup of coffee.

When everything is ready and he is happily tucking into his food, I slide the key over to him. Monty freezes, fork halfway to his lips, and stares at the key like it's a snake that might bite him. "What's that?"

"A key to my place. So you can come by anytime you want. If I only get to be your Daddy while Adventures is closed, I want to make the most of my time with you, boy. You don't have to use it. But I want you to understand how serious I am about wanting you here as much and as often as you want to be here. Okay?"

"You can't say things like that." He sets down his fork, ignores the key, and climbs onto my lap, straddling me and kissing me all over my face. I hold him steady as his kissing turns to grinding against my lap. My dick is all for letting him hump me until we both come again. Then Monty rests his palms on my shoulders, right where my sunburn from the other day is already sore. I wince and pull back. Monty gives me an apologetic glance.

"Sorry, Daddy." He sits still, like he thinks I'm going to be mad. I'm not, but he's going to be late for work if we keep kissing and dry humping instead of eating and getting ready.

"Hush, it's fine." I ease him off of my lap. "You need to eat before you go, though. And I don't want to make my boy late."

Monty sits back in his chair and picks at his food.

"Don't you like your breakfast?"

"Huh? No, that's not it. The eggs taste good, thanks." Monty shovels in a big bite and chews, as if to prove his words true. I watch him as we eat our meals. Monty keeps glancing at the key on the counter and then at my face, like he's looking for a catch or a trick. There isn't one. I just don't see the point in taking it slow when he's what I want and I enjoy spending time with him.

"Take the key, I really am sure I want you to have it. I want to see as much of you as I can this summer, my Montysaurus. You said you wanted Daddy to take care of you, right?"

"Yeah."

"Well, I can spoil you better in person." I shrug.

"I think you missed the part where I'm already a spoiled brat." Monty drags his fork through a blob of melted cheese on his plate.

"Hardly. You're trouble, for sure, but you absolutely deserve someone to spoil you silly."

"And you really want me to come for dinner Wednesday?" Monty sounds skeptical, one eyebrow raised, as if he expects me to have gotten my fill after one measly weekend. That's a joke. I doubt I'll ever have enough of him now that I've scratched the surface. But promising him forever will only sound like a line, so I play it cool.

"Sure. You can even come back tonight, if you want. I assumed you might want an evening on your own after spending the entire weekend here. But if you're up for more tonight, let me know and I'll prepare dinner for two."

"I can do dinner. I should probably go home after, though."

"Whatever you want. Like I said, you're welcome to come and go as you please." I nudge the key closer to him. Monty takes it, closing his fist around the key like it's something precious.

"I might take you up on that, literally. The coming before I go part, I mean." He flutters his lashes at me playfully.

"That's my naughty boy." I lean in to kiss his forehead and tug his long queue of hair. "Let's get the dishwasher loaded and then you should leave."

"Oh, Daddy wants me to do chores now?" Monty flutters his lashes at me.

"Yep." I agree. Monty shrugs and slides off his seat to help me tidy the kitchen. We get the job done with him teasing me all the way. At one point, he bends over while nominally loading the dishwasher. He plays it up, taking far longer than our two plates require, waggling his ass at me and giving me fuck me eyes over his shoulder. I give him a gentle swat that has him moaning like a porn star.

If we weren't running late, I might have let him goad me into a more thorough spanking. Or a quickie in the kitchen. Instead, I gather my boy in my arms, pressing his back to my chest so I can whisper filthy promises in his ear. "Teasing me when we don't have time to act on it is going to get you your ass blistered and thoroughly fucked tonight, baby boy. You remember that in your cubicle at work today, alright?"

"Yes, Daddy." Monty squirms around in my arms to kiss my face. "I can't wait."

"Well, for every minute you're late to work, you're going to wait an hour longer for your spanking tonight." I give him a conniving grin.

That lights a fire under him and we finish up with the dishes in record time.

When I kiss him goodbye in the entryway, he clings to me like I'm his universe. Yep, this boy is trouble, alright, exactly the sort of trouble I can't wait to keep getting into.

CHAPTER 13

Monty

I t might say something about how much time I've been spending with Daddy that it jars me to realize I have plans without him this weekend. It's Saturday, the day my friends usually meet up outside of the kink scene. I've skipped the last several weeks, okay, nearly three months, in favor of spending every spare moment with Daddy. So my friends would get annoyed if I bailed today, too.

This get together is for our monthly D&D session. For the third month in a row, we are meeting at Harry's instead of Adventures, since the club is still in the midst of renovations. Which means I've got to dump out the bag of clothing and toiletries that I've been bringing with me to Daddy's all summer long to make room.

Daddy offered me a drawer to use. I should consider taking him up on that with the amount of time I spend at his place lately. But then it might destroy me to clean out that drawer at the end of the summer. Better not to think about that and focus on stuffing snacks into my empty bag.

The stockpile of jerky and soda I bought on my way home from dinner at Daddy's place last night to share with everyone barely fit. Snacks make a good bribe to get my buddies off my back about how busy I've been wringing the most out of my temporary relationship.

I tuck my character sheet and dice into the front pocket, replacing the box of special condoms I picked up on my way to Daddy's last night. We blew through the last box with all the fucking we've been doing. I probably shouldn't be spending most of my nights at his place if I want to keep things casual. A light and breezy summer fling does not include the keys to his place and nightly sleepovers for going on three months. But I want him and he wants me, so where's the harm? Besides, he started it by giving me his key. He wouldn't have done that if he didn't want me there.

I sigh, knowing the harm comes at the rapidly approaching end of the summer when this all ends and I'm back to being alone. Only it will be so much worse to be alone after having a taste of the type of relationship I crave. Daddy takes care of me so well. It might be a tossup whether I'll miss the phenomenal sex or the world-class daddying more when this ends.

Who am I kidding? It's Luke I'm going to miss. Luke with his gentle touches. His confident control of my body with his ropes. His calm corrections when I step out of line. The way he can spank me until I'm writhing in pain, take me right to the brink of too much, and then fuck me like I'm irrevocably his.

I text Daddy to tell him I'm heading to Harry's to meet my friends for our monthly D&D session. He asks me to text or call when I get home. So I promise that I'll text him later as I head downstairs to catch a ride with Tate.

My best friend is waiting in front of my building. Huh, Tate's on time for once. He takes one look at my dreamy smile as I read the return text I just received from his brother, and I can tell I'm going to spend the entire drive dodging questions.

Tate's been nosy about my secret daddy the last few times we chatted. Which is rich, considering there have been a few times I've caught him sounding fucked out and breathless, or calls where he seemed like he was on the edge of coming down from his little head space, but I haven't pried for fear he'd want reciprocity and I'm not ready to spill the beans to Tate about my arrangement with his brother.

"So, are you going to tell me who has your social calendar completely booked the past few months, Monty?" Tate demands as soon as I slide into the passenger seat.

Tate turns to face me, hands on his hips like a stereotypical parent catching a curfew-dodging teen. Not my parents. I never had a curfew. Mom loves me, but she isn't the type to show it with strict rules and hovering.

Daddy Luke, though, he's the type to punish me for breaking a rule. He's gotten good at creative punishments over the past couple of months. After that first time, when I had a breakdown over my corner time, none of those punishments include withholding his presence from me. He might make me wait for what I want. Or deny me an orgasm for a night or two, but he hasn't made me go away or shown any signs of getting sick of me.

I wonder what he'll do if I forget to check in with him after our game tonight. Part of me is tempted to see. Push my limits and his buttons. That's for later, though. For now, I'm here to play with my friends, not dwell on all the things I want to do with Daddy while I've got him in my life.

"I've just been playing with a new daddy I met." I buckle my seatbelt, trying to look nonchalant about it. No big deal. "We're making the most of the summer sunshine."

That makes Tate bust up laughing. "Oh! that reminds me." He digs into his pocket for his phone and pulls up his social media. Tate hands me the phone. "Look at my brother's new profile pic. It appears he found a summer fling to enjoy the sun with, too." Tate makes a suggestive face at me as he pulls his car into traffic. We head toward Harry's place as I take in the image of Daddy Luke's bare chest. Tate is referring to the picture of my handprints on Luke's pecs, clearly outlined in sunburned skin. He took the picture ages ago. Weird that he's uploaded it online now, but whatever. It must have been an impulsive thing while he was updating his socials.

When I left his place last night, Daddy was going through the summer's pictures. He posted several albums in his private ropes group to show off images from his latest suspension workshop with Angel from last month. When I asked about all the new pics, he suggested getting a buddy of his to take some photos of me in suspension. Which sounds hot as hell, if it wouldn't be a visceral reminder of what I stand to lose when Adventures reopens next week. I'm trying not to think about it. Or the workshop Daddy is running the week after the annual Summer Fling party at Adventures.

The picture of Daddy Luke, beaming and burnt, still reminds me of my residual guilt about that day. No matter how many times Daddy tells me he isn't mad about it. I should have paid better attention. His chest is just so distracting. All of him is, really. Memories of our first beach day make me smile, despite my guilt.

I lick my lips as I peruse my daddy's naked torso. "He's so hot," I blurt before I remember we aren't supposed to be broadcasting our relationship to the world. Besides which, Tate knows I'm seeing someone.

"You aren't exclusive with your summer daddy?" Tate glances at me while we sit at a red light.

"I mean, I might not be entirely single, but I can still enjoy the view, right?" I joke with a weak laugh. He's making me squirm. Or that might be the guilt at keeping secrets from my best friend for the first time ever.

"I suppose." Tate doesn't sound convinced. He looks pensive. So I make an abrupt subject change, speculating over our other friends' relationship statuses and whether Harry will attend the next little night Kylee and Quent are hosting. Tate lets the subject drop.

When we get to Harry's place, we have to circle the block a few times to find parking. We end up being the last to arrive, but no one seems to mind. They're all hanging out and goofing around for a bit before Harry gets started, anyway.

Tate and I take a seat at the table with the others. I rummage in my bag for my contribution to the array of snacks already sitting in the middle for whoever wants them.

"So, you never said if you were exclusive with your new mystery daddy," Tate brings up my relationship again. I choke on my spit, even though I should have realized he'd never let the topic go so easily.

"We are. But it's just casual, like I said. Just a bit of summer fun while Adventures is closed."

"So, he's a member?" Connor asks. Crap. I didn't mean to tell them that. It might narrow the dating pool enough for them to put the pieces together. Especially if they notice my rope burns. But, no, plenty of tops like to play with rope. They shouldn't question the marks. Especially since everyone here knows how much bondage helps to clear my racing mind.

"Um, maybe? Anyway, I can have a fling without making it a big thing." I chomp on a carrot to occupy my mouth and keep from revealing anything else I don't intend to give away.

"You can… " Tate gives me an expectant look, but I ignore the long pause that I'm certain he's hoping will draw me into spilling the beans about my mystery daddy. Another carrot helps me maintain my silence. Tate knows me well enough to realize that waiting me out is a solid tactic. But I'm ready to resist. Daddy and I agreed to keep things low key. For once, I want to be good.

Tate sighs, and turns his attention to showing the others Luke's sunburn photos on his phone.

"Ugh. Not fair. Why are all the best daddies always taken?"

Connor grumbles.

"You mean Daddy Luke? But you don't even like bondage," I point out defensively before I can think it through. Doh. I dart my gaze to Tate. He's watching me speculatively, so I need to change the subject. "I'm sure you'll find your dream daddy when you least expect it, Connor. Have you had much luck with that new app you mentioned?"

"It's not an app, it's a new local meetup group on Fet. They're doing an in person event, but I'm not sure I'm going."

"Why not?" I ask. "You can't expect to meet your daddy if you don't put yourself out there, Con."

"I could go with you, if you need moral support," Quent offers. "Mommy won't mind."

"I can come too," Tate offers. "We could all go. Monty, you said this new relationship of yours is just a summer fling, right? You could tag along and look for something with long-term prospects."

"No!" I say without thinking through how that sounds, and then I backpedal. "I mean, I've got a partner for now. It would be weird to go to a singles event when I'm not technically single. Daddy might not like it. I'd have to ask him, I guess."

The thought of having a daddy to ask permission for attending a kink event makes me downright giddy. Not that I *need* permission from Luke to do anything I want. But going to a singles mixer is probably something I should run by the guy I'm seeing regardless of our power dynamic, right? To be certain we're on the same page about how serious things are between us, if for no other reason.

The truth is, though, I don't want to go. I don't want to meet new potential partners when I've been sleeping with the perfect guy for me for months now. I wouldn't trade in what Daddy and I have for anything. It's him I want, not some generic daddy who ticks all the boxes on some checklist. I want Luke and only Luke. Yeah, I've got it bad.

My friends are all excitedly chattering about the event and what they are hoping to find at the mixer. Even Harry is getting in on the action, describing his perfect, less than kinky, match. Though, oddly, he seems to like the idea of a man who can throw him around some. A man who will pin him down, pull his hair and make him come buckets. Sounds kind of primal. And hot.

Sort of reminds me of a couple nights ago when Daddy gave me a mid-week reward. He put me in a hip harness and suspended my ass about a foot above his bed so he could fuck and spank me at his leisure. It was so hot to be bound and at his mercy while he took his time with me. If I squirm just right in my seat, I can still feel the delicious ache of it in my ass. I want more of that.

Tate is still watching me, so I wink at him. I don't care if he notices how well-fucked I've been lately. There is only so much I'm willing to hide from my best friend and we share pretty much everything.

Harry gets the game going after the excitement about Connor's meetup ramps down. When I get out my dice to start the game, one of the polyurethane condoms I had stashed in my bag flops out onto the table. It must have fallen out of the box. No big deal. I scoop up the foil packet to put it away.

"Someone's been getting laid, huh, Monty?" Connor ribs me about it. "Or is that aspirational?"

"I built it so my new daddy will *come*," I agree with a broad wink.

Quent and Connor chuckle and offer me fist bumps. I dole them out to both of my friends, then stuff the condom back into my bag for later.

I glance at Tate, hoping he didn't notice or recognize the telltale branding. It's not like Luke is the only man in the world with a latex allergy. He can't recognize who my daddy is based on a quick glimpse of a condom wrapper. Tate doesn't comment, so I figure I've dodged that bullet.

"That's the horny pre-teen style humor I've come to know and expect from my players. Are we ready to begin?" Harry asks from behind his laptop screen. He has PDFs of all the rulebooks on there, along with all the details of our campaign and characters.

"You love us." Quent sticks out their tongue at Harry.

"Eh, you're okay. I guess I'll keep you." He wobbles his hand in a so-so gesture.

"I am a treasure and a delight, and you know it." Quent sits up to their full height and puts on haughty airs. "Of course you want to keep me, but I've already got a mommy, so you'll just have to take that up with her."

"Watch that smart mouth of yours, pup." Harry shoots Quent a warning look.

Quent licks their lips, for all the world like they'd love to get their mouth on Harry's dick. They probably would. I've never met anyone as enthusiastic about giving head as Quent.

Harry picks up on what Quent isn't quite offering, too, from the way he shifts in his seat like he's trying to subtly adjust himself.

"We could always play a different game instead..." Quent trails off suggestively. They glance around to assess whether the rest of us would be on board with turning tonight into a play party. I'm torn. I wouldn't say no to Q blowing me while Miss Kylee calls the shots. Or coloring with Tate. It's been a couple of weeks since Kylee and Quent's last play party. We haven't done anything kinky together since then. And I enjoy playing the big brother to Tate and Connor when they're in their little headspace.

"Nope, dragons." Connor shakes his head and crosses his arms over his chest. "I've been waiting all month for dragons."

"D&D night." Tate nods firmly. "We'll have a play night soon, but tonight is for our game, Q."

"Much as I'd love to let you lick my dick, Q, I have to agree with the others," I say. Besides, playing with Quent is probably something I should get permission from Daddy for, right? If he was my forever daddy, that's exactly what I'd want, for him to give permission for me to play with other people. He did say I need permission to come, so playing with Quent probably counts. It sucks that our arrangement is temporary.

"Boo, you're no fun." Quent sighs dramatically. "Fine. Let's play."

"Alright, so we left off last time with your band of brave adventurers rescuing a group of goblins who got captured by a crusading paladin. Now that you have returned in triumph with the freed captives, the goblin king is throwing a feast in your honor... "

Harry recaps our previous exploits before letting us go to town on the feast. It's a particularly silly and lighthearted session and we have fun with it. I appreciate that I have to focus on the story too much to dwell on what I'm keeping from Tate and the others. We have a fun night, and when Quent offers me a quickie for the road, an offer I am usually happy to take them up on, I decline. I'd rather get out of here so I can text Daddy than let someone else suck me off. Not without Luke's approval. He might enjoy watching, though? That would be hot.

Not for the first time, I wish Adventures wasn't closed. Then again, losing access to the club got Luke to agree to be my daddy for the summer. Plus, Martin is promising to make the club better than ever before when it reopens. So it might not all be bad.

And with the club reopening soon, it makes my time with Daddy even more precious. I think he is as happy with our situation as I am, but all good things come to an end. Better to make a clean break when the club reopens than to cling on to my temporary daddy until he's completely sick of me, right? Right. I'll just have to make the most of my remaining time having a daddy to call my own.

CHAPTER 14

Luke

"Great, I'll send over the work summaries for you to invoice when I get home then." Tate agrees as we wrap up our daily check-in about the business on the Monday after he and Monty had their game night.

Monty came over after Tate dropped him off at his apartment and we spent the rest of the weekend wrapped up in each other. My boy rolling out of bed early to get to work this morning made me hate Mondays more than I have since I started working from home. One of the many perks of managing the business I share with Tate.

"Sounds good." I'm only half-listening as I skim over the appointment spreadsheet for the week and I've got all the billable hours up to date from what Tate has already reported. He's going to send me the audio recordings of his invoicing anyway to confirm everything, so this chat is a formality.

"Hey, listen, there's something I've been meaning to ask about." Tate sounds casual, but I tear my attention away from the computer screen and focus on the call. We haven't talked much about life outside work lately. I've been too wrapped up in the glow of a new relationship.

"Yeah? What's up, Tatey-Tot?" I tease him with an old family nickname. I'm one of the few people who can get away with calling him that. Tate always bristles about strangers using it. Monty is one of the few outsiders I've heard use a similar nickname for Tate without getting a major stink eye from my brother.

"Nothing big. I just noticed that you and Monty have both been busy an awful lot this summer."

"Mhm, is that so? We've been having glorious weather," I observe.

"Right. Monty loves the beach." Tate is clearly fishing.

"Plenty of people love the beach." I keep my tone noncommittal.

"Ugh, are you going to make me ask outright?" My brother's exasperation makes me smile. He's easy to get a rise out of sometimes. Mostly when he cares about something, and Monty is someone he loves like a brother, I understand that. It's why I was hesitant to play with Monty at first. I'm not hesitant anymore. I want Monty to be my boy for as long as he'll have me. Not just the summer or until the club reopens. Now I just need to convince Monty of that fact.

"I can't imagine what you're implying, Tate." I feign ignorance.

"You are infuriating, you know that? I wanted to assure you that you don't have to hide anything from me. I'm glad you've got Monty to push your buttons at least half as much as you push mine. The two of you could consider not hiding that you're together? You could come to one of Kylee's play parties as a couple. Or the Summer Fling when Adventures reopens next week?"

Well, Monty *did* say he didn't want to lie to my brother. "Thanks. I didn't think you'd mind. Monty doesn't believe I'll stick around, so he didn't want drama."

Tate sighs. "Yeah. That sounds like Monty. He's not half as brash as he seems when it comes to knowing his worth, huh?"

"We're working on it." I switch my phone to my other ear. "Was there anything else?" The last time I saw my brother at our moms' place he was acting cagey about what he's been up to all summer. Not my place to pry into his personal life, though. Even if he is asking about mine.

"No, that was it. I'm glad you two are happy together. You should both come back to playing with the group. I mean, unless public play isn't your thing anymore?"

"No, it's our thing. I mean, I'm still not into public sex, but everything else is on the table, so to speak. Are you sure you're alright with me in your space?"

"I've always been okay with it; you just caught me by surprise when you joined the club. It's not like I'm going to get off on watching my brother fuck my best friend, but that doesn't mean I don't want you both to enjoy yourselves. And Monty likes to be watched. So come to the club, or play parties to your heart's content. I can look the other way when you get frisky with your boy. It's not like either of you have anything I haven't seen before."

I chuckle at that. "That's my Tatey-Tot, eloquent as ever."

"I'm sticking my tongue out at you. And I'm going to hang up now. See you soon?" he asks.

"Yeah, see you soon, Tate. Dinner at my place next weekend? I'm thinking the Sunday, after the Fling."

"With you and your boy?" he checks.

"Yep."

"I'll be there if you can get Monty on board about telling everyone you two are together. He's right that I have no interest in getting dragged into the middle of drama."

We hang up and I finish my work for the day. I'll deal with transcribing the new batch of invoices in the morning. For now, I've got Monty coming over, and a workshop to prepare for next week. One that I still haven't finalized plans for because I need a model. Oh, and I need a grand romantic gesture to convince my boy to stay with me after Adventures reopens and our own personal summer fling comes crashing to an end.

CHAPTER 15

Monty

Summer Fling at Adventures is one of my favorite events. Part of that is because almost the entire membership attends most years. And this year I'm seeing a ton of fresh faces, too. New prospective members visiting and regulars bringing guests.

The event is packed and the renovations Martin made are worth the wait. Harry has outdone himself on the work. I can't believe it only took two months from when Martin hired him to transform the shabby club into something chic that better reflects the welcoming space it has become.

Now there is a dedicated lounge area where we can sit and grab non-alcoholic drinks and snacks. There is a proper stage for demos and all new furniture and finishes. The place looks better than I've ever seen it. Not that I didn't enjoy the comfort of walking in and feeling right at home here, but now everything looks sleek and professional. There's a trendy vibe that might attract new members.

Luke is here too, but I've been avoiding him tonight. The reminder that the club reopening means our time together is coming to a close will only take the magic out of the evening. I want to bask in the glow of seeing all my friends and knowing our haven is back, not dwell on what I'm losing.

And for a while, it works. Tate finds me in the crowd and we grab some of the sparkling juice Martin provided as a celebratory beverage of the night. We sip it in the lounge while we observe all the guests and catch up on recent gossip.

Tate dances around asking what I've been up to and his eyes track Luke's movements almost as close as mine do. My bestie seems almost as distracted as I am, but I'm too caught up in my own worries to begin to guess why. I don't like the jealous roiling in my stomach anytime a rope bunny approaches him. So when he comes into the lounge to get a drink for himself, I drag Tate back into the play area to look around.

We wander the space, examining all the new features. That gets my mind off Luke again. Until we run into Martin and he points out the brand new hardpoints that he had installed above the gorgeous new event stage. I've been teasing him about getting a proper setup for suspension bondage for ages. And doesn't it just figure that he'd put it in now, when I'm about to lose Daddy?

Seeing him examining the new hardware hits me like a punch to the gut, and I can barely focus on Martin as he introduces me to his new boy. Bobby. Cute little twinkie, I can see the appeal. The adoration in his eyes when he looks at Martin reminds me of how deep I've fallen for my daddy.

I put a cheerful mask on to hide how devastated I am about Luke potentially moving on from our relationship, such as it is. Now every time he does a demo using those brand new hardpoints, it will just be a reminder of what I let slip through my fingers. I should be excited, so I act like I am. From the concerned glances Tate shoots my way, I'm not fooling him, but Martin doesn't seem to notice anything is amiss.

Maybe I can convince Daddy to string me up in front of everyone we know as our last hurrah? I can't stand ignoring the problem or stewing about it any longer. I almost dash off without a second thought, but Daddy expects better manners from me. Even if I can't focus on chit chat with Martin or making friends with Bobby right now. I thank Martin, say goodbye to his cute new boyfriend, and jog through the crowd to talk to Daddy. The way I should've done from the moment he walked in tonight instead of avoiding him.

Daddy Luke is easy to find, admiring the new rigging area. A couple of rope bunnies he's played with in the past are standing with him, flirting. Angel and their wife, I think. Both rope bottoms, though Hope is Angel's domme when they aren't playing with rope bondage.

I've never been bashful about asking for what I want in a scene. But asking him to be mine in front of everyone? Claim me as his boy for more than a night or a demo? That's scary as hell.

I don't let my fear hold me back tonight. Instead of waiting on the outskirts to be noticed, I march right up to my daddy and wrap my arms around him from behind in a big bear hug.

"There's my boy!" Daddy chuckles when he realizes it's me. He turns his head toward me, offering me a greeting kiss at my interruption.

"Hi, Daddy," the words come out breathy and excited. I'm smiling so widely it makes my cheeks hurt. It's a relief that he is so warm with me right now. No matter how much I've tried to convince myself that he's different—that *we're* different—I've worried about how he'll treat me in public after our summer together. I was avoiding him earlier to put off being rejected.

Clearly I've played with too many guys who are a terrible match for me. This kind of greeting would irritate most of my exes. They each made it clear I was being bratty as hell to just flounce in and demand all of their attention, regardless of what they were doing or who they were with. But that's a part of me Daddy Luke always encourages. I'm not in my little space right now, but there are aspects of our dynamic that I want from my daddy all the time.

The care taking side of things, mostly.

And Daddy Luke isn't just into some static ideal of our roles, he's into me. Messy, needy, scatterbrained me. Complete with all the back-talking, begging, pleading, impulsivity, and demanding I can give him at my worst. And the sweeter moments we've shared are all the better for knowing he accepts the total package.

Daddy leans into my hug and pulls me around to face him when I loosen my grip.

"Are you enjoying your night, Monty?"

"Yes, Daddy." I nod and snuggle into his side, claiming my rightful place. He puts his arm around me, acknowledging that I have every right to be in his personal space in front of everyone. It's wonderful. Until the full impact of that realization hits me. This might feel natural, but I'm making a statement by showing this much affection to Daddy on the big stage, even if we aren't doing a scene.

Oh, shit. Tate is going to see this. I guess there's no more hiding. As if he hasn't already figured it out. The fact he stopped pestering me to tell him who I've been seeing after our game session tells the entire story. He knows, and he's respecting my right to decide on when to tell him. Well, I guess tonight. If Daddy wants to keep me. And if not, well Tate's my best friend, it'll be his shoulder I'm crying on if Luke rejects me now. Despite my best intentions, I don't think I can handle losing the best relationship I've ever had without my best friend's support. Tate will understand.

I screw up my courage and glance back toward where I left Tate chatting with Bob and Martin. I catch his eye and wiggle my fingers in a wave without letting go of his brother. Tate winks at me and flashes me a thumbs up before turning his focus back on his conversation. Yeah, he totally knew. And he's okay with this. That's a load off my mind.

"Oh, I didn't realize you were in a relationship," Angel

comments with a genuine smile. That draws my attention back to the conversation at hand.

"It's new, right, Monty?" Daddy presses a kiss to my temple. I let his warmth suffuse me. He's so good at giving me what I need. Like subtle reassurances that I'm his and he doesn't care who sees it.

"Yep." I agree. I like Angel, even though I don't know them well. They're a model Daddy works with a lot. They were the one who did the big workshop with him last month. The model who had to duck out of the demo the night Daddy tied me up in front of everyone the weekend before Adventures closed. In a way, I have that cancelation to thank for getting to know Luke better as a daddy dom. Angel and Hope both congratulate us.

"Guess that means your dance card is going to be fuller? Will we need to find a new rigger, Luke?" Hope teases.

Daddy glances at me, and I take a minute to realize he wants my input on this.

"Daddy can tie up whoever he wants, so long as I get to watch." I tip my head toward him. We talked about this when he agreed to play with me. I don't care who else he ties up so long as I'm the one in his bed afterward or turned over his knees for a spanking. Or better yet, both.

"That's right. And I'll be happy to take this new setup for a spin another night, when the club is less busy."

"You're on for that. Another night, then. It was lovely to catch up, dear. Keep in touch. And thanks for asking after Bethany. Her broken arm is just about healed now, but it sure put a damper on her summer." Hope squeezes Daddy's arm, and he pats her hand. So they were discussing Hope and Angel's pre-teen daughter when I burst in on them. Oops. I'm still not sorry. "We won't keep you from your boy." Hope gestures for Angel to follow her as she turns to leave.

"Talk to you later, Daddy Luke. Bye, Monty. I doubt you'll need my services as much for your workshops, but call me if you still need a model for next week," Angel offers.

"I will, thanks, Angel." Daddy waves at them as they go, then turns a questioning look toward me. "Well, I had intended to make a bit of a scene asking you to be mine tonight, but seeing as how you've already staked your claim, what do you say? Do I need to call Angel about the workshop?"

"Huh?"

"I'm asking you to be my model, naughty boy."

"Oh. Yes. I'd love that. You know how much I enjoy getting your ropes on me. It will be even better with an audience."

I bite my lip, considering my next question. It's hard not to blurt it out, since this has been on my mind for ages. I don't want to reflect badly on him and everyone in our circles knows me. They know I'm not well behaved. I can be bratty, but it's not just the willful play-acting that some daddies enjoy. It's not that I'm a brat who acts out to get punished, though that is also true. It's that I sometimes lack impulse control and struggle with basic commands.

The thing that no one I've played with before Daddy Luke has ever grasped is that my disobedience isn't always willful. Sometimes I want to obey and I just can't quite seem to make whatever Daddy asks of me happen. I can have a comprehensive list of things I want or need to do, have every intention of completing it, make a plan, set aside time, and then it still doesn't happen. My therapist calls it poor executive function. I call it a pain in the ass.

"Daddy?" I need to just ask him, even though it seems ridiculous since he just claimed me in front of two of his closest friends. In front of the entire club, really, since I wasn't exactly subtle with my greeting and he reciprocated enthusiastically.

"Yes, Monty?" he asks, guiding me away from the big demo

stage to let other people check out the new hardware.

"Are you going to tell them all that I'm your boy? At the workshop, I mean." I bite my lip, knowing I already as much as broadcast that information to everyone we know. Gossip travels fast in our community.

"Do you want me to?" He takes the question seriously.

"I'm not sure."

"We don't have to do anything you aren't ready for, Monty. I can just introduce you as my friend who volunteered to model for the evening, if that makes you more comfortable?"

It's weird that his suggestion fills me with both buoyant relief at getting a reprieve and crushing disappointment that he doesn't want to claim me in front of our community. "I guess we can do that. If you want."

I must not hide my hurt very well. Daddy hugs me tight. "I'd be happy to claim you in front of everyone if that's what you want, Monty."

"I'm just not sure if I'm ready. What if you change your mind?"

"That won't happen. I can't promise that our feelings for each other will never change, but I'm not going anywhere."

"Not even after the summer?"

"Nope. I've enjoyed our time together. Why would I let a silly time limit end that when we're both happy together?"

"You are?"

"Yes."

"Huh."

"I'd be thrilled to extend what we have indefinitely." Daddy pats my arms.

"You would?" I try not to sound incredulous, but I'm not sure I succeed.

"Yes." Daddy brushes his fingers over my cheek with a sad smile. "Of course I would."

"Because I'm behaving better?" I ask, unable to conquer my more insidious fears completely.

"No." Daddy stops and turns to face me. He cups my chin in his palm and tips my face up for a gentle kiss. "It's because you're you and I care about you, silly boy."

"Oh. I care about you too, Daddy." To prove it, I kiss him again, with my arms wrapped around his neck.

"I love you, my Montysaurus." Daddy breathes the words against my lips. God, I want to drag him off to one of the private rooms so he can ravish me. Tonight is more of a social event, so there isn't much public play going on in the common areas.

"I love you, too, Daddy." It's hard to tear my lips away from his long enough to say the words back to him, but I manage it. Then we get lost in each other's lips. We separate after a long passionate kiss to a scattering of catcalls.

"Does all of this mean you're ready to tell people? Like Tate?" Daddy asks when I let him come up for air. He's laughing and disheveled and that only makes me want him all to myself even more, but I nod.

"Yeah. We can shout it from the rooftops if you really want to, Daddy."

"I want to. You're mine. And that being the case, you won't mind having Tate over for a family dinner tomorrow night, right?"

I swallow hard. Family dinner implies that I'm part of his family now. That's a degree of permanence I've never let myself hope for before. I want it. With Luke, I want everything.

"I love you," I repeat the words. "I don't care who knows it."

Daddy responds by kissing me again, maneuvering me against a wall in an out of the way alcove next to one of the private rooms. The room is already in use when we separate enough to try the door. We find an unoccupied low couch off to the side where we can kiss and grope to our heart's content while we wait for whoever is using it to finish.

I'm too interested in tasting Daddy's lips to mind the delay. Our make-out session only builds the excitement over what we'll get to do once we get some privacy. His mouth on mine is the sweetest thing in the world.

Too bad we can't fuck right here on the couch, where anyone could watch us. Mm, I love the idea of riding Daddy's cock out in the open. Most nights, that wouldn't be an issue, but with the catered party in full swing all around us, full nudity and penetrative sex are frowned upon. Besides, Daddy isn't into it. Which is fine. I don't care where he fucks me, so long as he does.

We can wait for a private room. Daddy loves me. He isn't going anywhere and we'll have plenty of time to fuck on every surface in the newly reopened club now that he's agreed to keep me. This is the best Summer Fling ever.

CHAPTER 16

Luke

Monty came home with me after we left the Summer Fling at Adventures last night. It wasn't a decision that required much discussion. There was no way I was sleeping apart from him on the night we declared our love.

It's still sinking in that he's mine, no time limits or deadlines looming over us. Monty is my boy and I'm his daddy for keeps. Tate was a smart ass about it when we spoke to him after our celebration in one of the private rooms at the club.

I'm hoping he'll behave tonight, but knowing my brother, that's doubtful. The plan is to bribe him into good behavior with his favorite meal. I called our moms for their eggplant parm recipe and I've been toiling away in the kitchen half the day to make sure it's just like they always make it. A big saucy casserole served over fresh spaghetti from the market next to the wine store.

Monty cajoled me into getting a few bottles of his and Tate's favorite sparkly sweet wine. It didn't take much more than the boy batting his lashes at me. I'm a pushover and I don't even care.

Monty isn't the sort of bratty that requires a firm hand. What my boy needs is plenty of attention and affection to bring out his sweet side. Like today, he helped me run errands, grab groceries, and prepare our meal. All with none of his typical backtalk or acting out. He still gave me some lip about my wine preferences, but I like his snarky attitude. And now he's sitting at the counter watching me arrange the finishing touches to our meal while we wait for our guest.

"So, I get he knows about us, but do you think Tate will be mad when we tell him we've been together all summer?" Monty worries at his lip.

"He already knows. I'm not certain when he figured it out, but he called last week and invited me to tell him before the Fling. I'd have mentioned it to you, but I didn't want to spook you before I asked you to be mine on a more public and permanent basis."

"Yeah, that might have spooked me."

"I still don't understand why, baby. Have I done anything to make you think I'm less than all in with you?"

"No. You haven't. I guess I'm just used to being too much of a handful." He winks at me, making it a joke. But I get it. I've seen the way he flits from partner to partner at club events.

And I've heard people talk about his inability to follow orders. We've worked around that this summer. The problem isn't Monty; it's rigidly expecting him to follow some predetermined script instead of letting him be himself. Strict rules and the not so fun type of punishments don't work for us. It only took our first weekend together for me to figure out that much.

Monty is playful, and I can keep him in hand with the promise of a reward better than a punishment. Still, knowing all the gossip about him, it's easy to understand his hesitation about believing in anything serious. I hastily drain the finished pasta, turn off the burner, and go around the counter to hug him.

"You aren't. You just needed to find the right daddy for you."

"I needed you." Monty looks at me with so much heat and adoration that if Tate wasn't on his way, I'd drag my boy back to our bed and make love to him. But it might be awkward for my brother to arrive while I'm balls deep inside of his best friend, so sex will have to wait.

Sure enough, just as I'm contemplating whether we have time for a quickie, Tate calls my phone.

"Hello? Are you running late?" I tease. He's got a habit of not being the most punctual outside of work hours.

"Nope, not this time, just called to inform you that I'm out front so you and Monty can get decent."

"We are." I say dryly. "Door's unlocked, come on inside." I hang up, set my phone aside and kiss Monty's temple. "Ready?"

"Yes, Daddy."

"Good. Go greet our guest while I set the table." I ruffle his hair.

Monty beams at me, then hops up to go greet Tate. I give his ass a gentle smack as he passes me in a promise of things to come. Monty gives me a happy little moan in reply and shoots me a wink over his shoulder. Before he can get more than a step away, the door opens and my brother calls out a tentative greeting.

"Hello? You two didn't run off to screw as soon as I called, did you?" Tate teases as he toes off his shoes and leans past the entryway to see into the open kitchen area.

"Nope. Check out what we made." Monty drags Tate into the kitchen area to present the meal we prepared, clearly proud of his contributions to our dinner.

Tate makes an appreciative sound. "Oh, wow, you two went all out, huh? Are you trying to buy my approval with the moms' best recipe, Lucas?"

"You caught me." I wink at him.

Tate laughs. "You didn't have to go to the trouble. I already think you two are good for each other. You've both been weirdly smiley this summer. Though I never realized Monty had it in him to mark his daddy quite so dramatically. That sunburn picture was a look." He nudges Monty with his elbow and Monty gives him a shove back. Tate might mean it all in fun, but Monty is still sensitive about the sunburn incident and I try to catch my brother's eye to warn him off the topic. He doesn't notice.

"Hey! That was an accident, and I felt super bad about it." Monty crosses his arms over his chest and pouts.

"You accidentally felt my brother up instead of actually putting sunscreen on him?" Tate ribs him. "How does that work?"

"It just sort of happened." Monty flails his hands as he talks. "In my defense, have you seen his chest? And it was, like, the first time I had permission to touch him all over. What sort of superhuman self-control do you think I have? Anyway, I apologized and made it up to Daddy."

"I just bet you did." Tate imbues the words with a world of innuendo and adds a suggestive wink for good measure.

"You really are totally fine with this," Monty says the words like he hardly dares to believe them.

"Yes, Monty. I am happy that two of my favorite people are happy. I've known for a while now." Tate claims a hug from my flustered boy. "And you're still my best friend, even if you *do* end up being my step-brother-in-law some day."

Monty wrinkles his nose. "That sounds weird."

"You're weird." Tate sticks his tongue out at Monty. "I still love you, though. I see you aren't disputing the part about wanting to marry my brother?"

Monty reciprocates by sticking out his tongue, which earns his ass a gentle swat from me for general rudeness.

"Behave, boy." I remind him in my mildest tone. My smile belies the warning. I appreciate seeing Tate and Monty acting silly together.

Then the rest of what my brother said seems to sink in and Monty flails his arms again. "Hey wait, what? No! It's *way* too soon for wedding bells." Monty glances at me to confirm that.

There's a nervous expectation in his eyes that makes me think he wouldn't hate it if I contradicted that statement. He's right though; we just said I love you for the first time. It's premature to talk about formal promises of forever. Still, a part of me aches for him to want that with me. "Right?" Monty prompts me when I take too long to reply.

"Right. For now. We'll revisit the idea at a later date." I wink at him, hoping to convey that I want us to have that kind of permanence in our future. Monty flashes me a relieved grin. We can discuss what our future looks like later, in private, but I suspect Tate is correct that my boy would revel in the pomp and ceremony of an actual wedding some day. A formal claim on my boy in front of witnesses.

"Cool, but mark my words, you two are both the type for all the romance. One of us ought to give our moms something like a traditional relationship, because I have no plans of walking down any aisles, ever." Tate insists.

That's my brother, cutting right to the chase and trampling over personal boundaries. There's a reason he and Monty get along so well. Tate doesn't give us time to reply. He turns all his attention to the food like he didn't just open a can of worms.

"But, just so you both know, I am obligated to warn you that if either of you breaks the other's heart I will kick his ass. And I won't be happy about it. You better not make me choose between the two of you. Or else. Now, let's chow down before all this deliciousness gets cold. It would be a sacrilege to let eggplant parm get all sad and soggy."

With that, Tate makes himself at home, grabbing the oven

mitts from my counter. He carries the pan of eggplant parm to the table, expecting Monty and I to follow with the other dishes. The rest of the day goes better than I expected and I can relax and enjoy having two of the people I love most together in my home. No more hiding or denying what I want.

CHAPTER 17

Monty

I let myself in when I arrive at Daddy's place the night of the workshop. Since the door that leads to his office is closed, I know he's already done with work for the day. I toe off my shoes and go searching for my daddy. Luke is in the kitchen fussing over the snacks for the workshop guests.

"I'm home." I saunter into the kitchen and lean against the counter to watch him work.

Daddy flashes me a huge grin. "Hey, Montysaurus, are you ready for tonight? I'm just putting the finishing touches on this."

"Yeah. Took my lunchtime dose of my meds so I should be all good. I'm excited." I snag a canape from a tray and roll my eyes at him when he shoots me a reproving glance for messing up the arrangement. With someone else, I might jump to conclusions about the reasons for his irritation. By now I'm familiar enough with Daddy to realize that his exasperation is purely at my messing with his snack presentation. "No one is coming to ogle the snacks, Daddy."

"That doesn't mean they don't appreciate the details. We eat with our eyes first." The way his eyes rove over me leaves me with no doubt he intends to devour me later. "Anyway, it's easier to concentrate on learning if you aren't hungry."

"Sure, I guess." I shrug and pop my purloined pastry puff into my mouth. It's got some sort of meat filling that tastes delicious. Maybe his hors d'oeuvres aren't the worst idea. I grab another one, this time a bite-sized quiche.

"You do a better job holding still for me when you've had a light meal before we play." Daddy points out knowingly as he nudges another couple of the snacks he hasn't plated yet toward me. The array of bite-sized appetizers from the frozen food aisle isn't exactly my definition of light, fried or wrapped in various forms of pastry, but it is delicious.

"That's true. I guess I should help myself then, since I'm going to be your model tonight, right?"

"You should." Daddy finishes arranging a fruit platter, washes his hands and comes around the counter to kiss me in greeting.

"Mm, well that's no hardship, your meat always tastes amazing." I flutter my lashes at him. My antics make Daddy snort in amusement, so I push the double entendre further. I have some restraint in that I paw at his crotch instead of rubbing my ass against him. "Can't wait to get this big juicy sausage roll in my mouth."

"Is that so?" Daddy takes my hand and presses it more firmly against his erection. Do we have time for a blow job before the workshop? I glance at the clock. No, probably not.

"Yes. You *did* say it's best not to play hungry and I'm ravenous for you, Daddy." I tease, running my free hand over his chest even as I continue rubbing him through his pants. He gives my ass an encouraging squeeze, and for a second I think he might give in to my seduction. But then he shakes his head and pulls away with a visible effort.

"Later. You can taste my meat to your heart's content after the workshop. For now, our guests could arrive at any moment and we still have to finish setting up the materials."

I pout at him, but he gives me a warning look, so I withdraw my hands. He's right. Not that I'd mind someone walking in on us. It's a kink event. Public sex isn't exactly a scandal at something like that. On the other hand, it's just a workshop. I guess the attendees might not reasonably expect to arrive in the middle of the instructor having his boy sucking his cock next to the refreshments. Okay. Right, other people might eat all the food that's laid out on our counter. I guess sex can wait until later.

"How was my boy's day?" Daddy's question pulls me out of my daydreams of sucking him off here in the kitchen. "Wash your hands before we finish setting up everything."

I shrug and we both scrub our hands. "My day was alright. Work was boring. I was too excited about tonight to focus."

"You always enjoy an audience." Daddy pats his hands dry, then turns back to arranging the final platter of assorted snacks.

"Yeah. I want to show off my Daddy's mad skills."

"We will. And I'll get to show them all how beautiful my naughty boy is." He beams at me like I truly make him proud to claim me. That is going to take more getting used to.

"I'm still a little nervous," I admit.

"What about, baby boy?"

I shrug and shuffle from foot to foot. "That you might change your mind, I guess. When I screw something up again."

"Not happening, Monty. You're mine." Daddy reaches over to tip my chin up so that I have to look at him. I'm nervous about meeting his gaze, but when I do, I can see his sincerity.

"Yeah, you say that now, but I know this is important to you. You've got paying customers and the fancy photographer for that kink blog coming, so don't pretend it's no big deal. What if I ruin the workshop? I could freeze up or be a total space case." I can't quite give up my fears. Daddy Luke has never given me any reason to believe he's anything like my past partners. The ones who made me feel like I'd never be good enough for someone to want me long-term.

Daddy leans toward me and rests his hands on my shoulders, setting aside his last-minute preparations to reassure me. That shows me as clear as anything that he cares. I'm his top priority when I need him. When he turns his full attention on me like this, those old voices telling me I'm not good enough fade to background noise and all I hear is him.

"First of all, Jackson is a friend. If you aren't comfortable with him photographing you, then I can reschedule the shoot with him for the next time Angel is available to model. Unless you've changed your mind about me tying up other people?"

"No, I don't care about sharing that. There's a dearth of skilled riggers and I like people knowing that my daddy has mad skills and he's generous with sharing them. So long as I'm the only boy who gets to call you daddy and join you in your bed, we're good."

"You're the only boy I want in my bed and calling me Daddy, my Montysaurus."

"Okay. Good. Because we sort of went public in front of the entire club and it would suck to walk that back so soon. I'm still nervous about screwing up your workshop, though. You know how I get sometimes."

"I do. Tell me, are you planning on ruining my workshop, Monty?" Daddy asks.

"No." I shake my head vehemently. "I wouldn't do that. It's important to you."

"It is. And I understand you wouldn't mess up on purpose. If something goes wrong, then we can address it. But whatever happens, I know you'd never try to ruin this for the fun of it," Daddy says.

"You do?" I can't keep the surprise from my voice. I'm still not used to a partner having faith in me, but I could get used to this trust we share.

"Yes, boy. Don't forget, I know you now. If you have a hard time focusing, we can do those visualizations that help center you before we move on with anything. Or take a break to stretch. Or change which ties we're demonstrating to better suit the mood."

"That won't ruin it?"

"No. It can enhance the learning experience. Part of being a good rigger is reading how your bottom is responding and knowing when they've had enough. Learning to be flexible about the plan is a valuable skill. Sometimes the perfect scene is a complex series of artistic ties that flow through a dynamic suspension and sometimes it's as simple as a utilitarian chest harness to ground you. Sometimes a bottom can't hold the pose I want for as long as I want. You wouldn't be the first to need a change of plans. The ability to rethink a scene on the fly is an important part of doing what we do safely. We're all only human. It stands to reason, adapting to the other human you are playing with is a valuable skill for me to teach, too."

"Okay. Good. That, uh, helps. Thanks, Daddy."

"I'm glad. Is there anything else worrying you?"

I purse my lips, considering. "No. I still want to make you proud, though."

"You do," Daddy leans in to peck me on the lips. "All the time. I'm so proud I get to call you mine. You're my perfect boy, Monty. Now, let's get ready to show some new friends just how wonderful you are."

It could sound like trite flattery, meant to assuage my fears, but coming from my daddy, I believe every word.

***

By the end of the workshop, I'm certain of two things. The first is that Angel is welcome to do the modeling for these things with Daddy. Turns out the demo we did together earlier in the summer was no fluke. I struggle to get my head into a scene when my dom is in teacher mode.

The other thing is that my daddy meant it when he said I didn't have to be perfect to be perfect for him. I spend most of the session fidgeting and fussing as he slows down each step and talks through the variations on various harnesses. Daddy sprinkles the entire session with safety tips. I keep earning little reminder swats to my ass to hold still. It's excruciatingly frustrating, because if it weren't so boring, his touches would have me sporting wood in my snug yoga shorts.

I get why he includes that stuff. What we do can be dangerous, but it's just so boring to hear about rope safety when I'm eager for him to make me fly. The only times I settle into the moment are when he runs his hands over my body to check that the ropes aren't pinching any nerves or restricting my circulation. During those frequent check-ins, he has his full attention on me, and I can relax into his care. He explains what he's doing to our audience as he touches me and watches my face. His tender touches make it clear I'm the center of his world while I give myself over to him and his ropes.

Daddy asks if I'm ready to go up, and it kills me to shake my head no, but I don't think I can handle that intensity tonight. He ends up only doing a partial lift instead of the full suspension we had planned because I'm too distracted for anything more intense than that. So much for my meds magically fixing my troubles. They make it easier to concentrate, but my nerves about performing well tonight seem to be too much for even medication to overcome completely.

It sucks to feel like a failure as I balance on one foot. I let the ropes cradle me when Daddy hoists one of my knees upward.

He wraps a quick double column tie from my knee toward my ankle and groin, making the partial suspension more artistic. I wallow in my disappointment with myself as I hold the pose for our audience. When he's happy with my bondage, Daddy stands protectively close in case I need to get down. He talks me through a quiet meditation when my fidgeting makes me wobble and strain.

Daddy's photographer friend, Jackson, snaps photos of me. That makes me focus on pushing the pose, really leaning into it with every breath and showing off Daddy's work. Daddy talks to me throughout that part. His intense scrutiny, coupled with the strain of holding my pose, finally lets me sink into the mental space I usually find during a scene.

Jackson shoots Daddy a thumbs up and then Daddy Luke goes back into teacher mode, showing everyone the finer points of his rope work and taking questions. He deflects an intrusive question about my weight by calmly explaining how it's important to work with your partner's body, not against it. Daddy segues into body positivity and how my size means he can use more wraps to stabilize the ropework and he can emphasize my sexy curves. He punctuates his praise for how irresistible I look, all trussed up, with a sharp slap to my ass. The smack has me moaning and swaying against the ropes holding me upright.

"Daddy," I protest, more because I want his attention than anything. Another spank would be nice, though. I want his marks all over me.

"How are you holding up, Monty?" Daddy checks in as he rubs a hand over my ass cheek.

"Okay." I try to wriggle against his touch, but it only makes me shift and dangle from the chest rope until I can catch my balance again.

Daddy steadies me. "Are you alright balancing for a moment longer?"

"If I get a spanking after," I agree, putting on my usual cheeky facade. My comment elicits a few chuckles from the crowd. For a second there, I almost forgot we had an audience.

"Hm, have you earned that, my boy?" Daddy teases.

"Yes." I nod and almost lose my footing again. I don't really think I deserve a reward, but I want him to hold me close and remind me I'm his.

"I think so, too. Now, keep it up a little longer for me. I'm going to show them how to lower you down to the mat and untie everything. Then you can snuggle up with some Gatorade while I go over some ropework with our guests, sound good?"

"Yes, Daddy." I agree. It's nothing to me. I'm still floating, so I barely notice anyone but Daddy until it's time for him to let me down.

Once I'm untied, Daddy tells the attendees to help themselves to the snacks while he snuggles me until I'm steady enough to go wait in our room for him. My role is over, but Daddy still has to handle the portion of the night where the attendees practice tying harnesses of their own. I know he isn't letting them do any suspensions today. Most of the attendees are newer to ropework, so I won't miss anything exciting if I retreat to his bed while he finishes doing his thing as an instructor.

I spend most of the wait moping over everything I did wrong, so Daddy's wide grin when he joins me some time later surprises me. He scoops me into his arms.

"You were magnificent. I can't wait to show you the pictures that Jackson took. You're going to love them."

"Uh-huh." I can't hide my disbelief.

Daddy frowns. "I mean it, Monty. You were wonderful. Tonight went well."

"You had to change to a partial suspension."

"I did." He nods. "It was the right call for tonight."

"I failed you." I can't meet his gaze.

"Hey, no." Daddy tugs my hair to get my attention. "You didn't fail. We talked about this. Needing a change of plans isn't a failure. Being yourself isn't a failure, and struggling with things that are hard for you isn't a failure. I know you can't always focus for long periods. You told me when I was asking too much. You never lied or tried to hide your struggles from me. We worked around the problem together. And you looked gorgeous holding your pose for me. My perfect boy." Daddy grips my long queue of hair to hold me in place for a kiss.

At first, I don't believe him. I don't know if there are any words that can convince me as well as Daddy's lips on mine, hungry and demanding. The sincerity of his mouth on me leaves me defenseless and I melt into the kiss. His erection pressing against mine as he lowers himself over me and ruts our dicks together, speaks a thousand words. I shudder under him as he shows me just how much I turn him on. Daddy gives the most amazing kisses.

"I love you, Monty. I'm not going anywhere just because you got distracted." He mouths along my neck.

"You sure, cause I get distracted a lot." I arch to give him better access and he sucks a hickey onto my neck.

"That doesn't matter. Or rather, you matter more to me. Let me put it another way: it's my job to keep you engaged in our scenes, not your job to force your brain to work in ways it doesn't." Daddy insists. That echo of his constant refrain that it's his job to take care of me finally hits home.

It's my job to let him take care of me. I've gotten used to thinking that means if I can't give my daddy my fidget-free picture-perfect obedient surrender, I'm failing. But I might have been looking at it all wrong. Maybe letting Daddy take care of me includes acknowledging when I need him to adapt to my differences. I have no problem with him working around my folds when he ties me up, so why should working around my mental quirks be any different?

"You really don't see my issues as a problem, do you?" I ask, just to be sure.

"Not in the slightest." He brushes a tender kiss against my brow. "You're my boy, fidgets and all." He peppers more sweet kisses over my cheeks. "I enjoy the challenge of keeping you on your toes." He tugs on my queue to tip my head back again, tracing his fingers over my lips. He gazes at my mouth like he's imagining my lips wrapped around his cock.

"Oh, god, that's nice." I moan at the sense memory of him holding me in place by my long hair while he feeds me his dick. That's a favorite from our repertoire. Tonight, he holds me in place while he plunders my mouth with hot and heavy kisses. His tongue demands entry and fucks into me until I'm breathless and horny beyond reason.

"I love you, Monty." He declares his love between more scorching kisses. "Every part of you." He sounds so sincere and raw that I have no choice but to believe him. "You drive me wild, boy. Love you to the moon."

"Need you, Daddy." I pant when he lets me up for air.

"Then take me." Daddy Luke's hands press my wrists into the soft cuffs still attached to the bedframe from last night when we were both too tired for ropes. I squirm under him as he works his way down my body to my groin, kissing and licking me all over. His hot mouth is sweet torture around my cock as he teases me until I'm begging him for release. When he finally relents and rolls a condom onto my dick, I buck up into his touch and have to fight not to come too soon.

"That's it baby, you're so hard for Daddy. You're going to fuck me so good, aren't you?"

"Yes, daddy. Please."

Daddy chuckles. "Knew I could teach you manners with the right incentive," he teases.

I groan, my snarky response flying out of my head as he lines up my cock with his hole. "Oh, fuck. Daddy! That's so good." The heat of his body as he lowers himself onto me is unreal. He takes my dick slow and steady, his hips rolling in a sensual caress. Even as I enter him, he's in control. This is still him taking care of me. He'll always take care of me.

"That's it, hold still. Daddy's got you." He takes his time, gradually lowering himself all the way down, until I'm buried inside him to the hilt, trembling with the need to fuck up into him. I'm desperate to thrust, but then he leans forward to kiss me some more and I cede control again. He tastes like my arousal as his tongue enters my mouth and I relax under him, content to take whatever he gives me.

That's when he moves, riding me in a slow and steady rhythm that builds and builds to an indescribable peak. I love when Daddy takes me inside him like this. Love that even though I'm the one entering him, he's still the one fucking me. Daddy Luke is controlling the encounter and taking care of his boy. As he takes his pleasure, I let myself drift again, taking everything he has to give. Loving that I'm making him feel good, that he's using my dick to take himself right to the edge of his orgasm.

I love the way his face looks, clouded in pleasure. The way his clenching channel milks my orgasm right out of me, even as his hot spunk splashes over my belly and chest. His lips crash hard against mine as he moans my name in ecstasy. I love him. And even if tonight didn't quite go according to plan, he still wants me. Still loves me and is proud to put me on display as his boy.

Daddy Luke still wants to claim me. Make love to me. And maybe I can let myself believe he always will. It's easy to feel that fleeting connection while I'm high on endorphins from coming my brains out inside of him. A sexual connection has never been hard for me to find. What's rarer is for the intimacy to extend outside of sex or a scene. After the part where Daddy cleans me up and takes off my bindings. The part that's always been missing before is how my daddy takes care of me after our breathing returns to normal and the sleepy post-orgasm lassitude from snuggling fades.

His love is deeper than anything I've had with anyone else. It's in the way he gazes at me with nothing but love, even after I wake him up flopping around trying to get comfortable enough to sleep.

"You said you took your meds at lunch. Do you need your sleep aid, Montysaurus?" Daddy asks sleepily. It makes me all warm inside that he remembers what I said about taking a noon dose of my ADHD meds making sleep difficult for me.

"Yeah, probably. I can grab my Switch and play in the other room until I'm sleepy so I don't bother you." I offer, swinging my legs out of bed to go to the drawer he cleaned out for me to keep some stuff here. The tangible reminder that he's making room for me in his life makes me smile. Now that this isn't temporary, I love the reminder that I'm his. Each tentative step toward a future with Daddy Luke fills me with hope.

"Nope, stay in bed, I'll get what you need." Daddy stops me from getting up by pulling me into a fierce hug. The ache in my muscles from just sitting up to hug him reminds me of how much strain even bondage in a simple one-legged balance pose puts on my core muscles. I appreciate him taking care of me even more than usual in light of that soreness.

Daddy gathers my sleep aid, a cup of water and my Switch. He hands me the first two, waits until I'm done with the water to trade the empty glass for my Switch, then rejoins me in bed. Daddy snuggles me close. "Before you start your game, I wanted to show you something." He hands me his phone. I lay my game on my lap and take the device.

Daddy's message history with Jackson is open on the screen and my eyes go right to the thumbnail proofs from tonight. From the timestamp, Jackson sent them while Daddy and I were busy.

"It's me." I tap the image to enlarge it and the beauty Jackson captured takes me by surprise. I don't see a failure in these images. The boy in the pictures is beautiful in his submission, one foot standing strong, the other held up knee bent and bound, calf to thigh. I stand suspended with my daddy by my side, our attention completely focused on each other. This image was taken while Daddy talked me through a meditation. The love and trust between us in that simple black and white still shot speaks volumes that I might finally be ready to hear.

"It is. Do you see what I see there, my boy?" Daddy asks, cupping my jaw.

Daddy doesn't want me to change, he loves me as I am. It's a jarring thing to realize, but it makes me love him even more. Subjectively, this picture of him doting on me, and me submitting myself to him even when it's hard, means everything. And objectively, the picture has a cool artsy vibe; it's the sort of thing I could see us putting up on our wall someday. Because, yeah, I can see a future where Daddy and I pick out custom art for our shared walls. Just the thought makes me giddy.

"I think so."

"And what is that?"

"Your very good boy?"

"Exactly." Daddy kisses me softly.

"Mm. I love it. Do you think we could get a big copy of it to hang over our bed?" I ask on an impulse. Then I glance up at the bare patch of wall and cringe internally at the presumption of calling the bed ours. Just because I sleep here most nights doesn't make it officially ours. Before I can open my mouth to backpedal, Daddy shuts me up with another kiss. Neither of us is up for more than that again so soon, but it's nice to feel connected to him this way.

"I'll talk to Jackson about the picture. I was thinking that might be the perfect shot for over our bed, sweet boy. And when you're ready, we can talk about officially moving you in, but there's no rush. I'm happy to have you whenever you're able to stay over."

"My lease renews in a couple months, maybe I could make it official then?" I suggest.

"That sounds perfect." Daddy pats my thigh. "Think you can sleep now?"

"Nope. But if you're sleepy I can play my game until I can." I offer.

Daddy chuckles. "Want to snuggle while you play?"

"Yes, please." I agree. We wriggle around so that I can recline against his chest and soon Daddy's soft snores punctuate the catchy music from the cutesy animal game I've got loaded to help make me drowsy. It takes a while to tire myself out with mindless video games in bed until my sleep aid kicks in and I can drift off to dreamland.

Daddy Luke isn't in bed with me when I blink groggily awake the next morning, but the smell of bacon and toast assures me he hasn't gone far. My console is docked on its charger instead of lost in the blankets where it might have tumbled to the ground. I smile at that little gesture. My daddy takes amazing care of me. It's all the small things that make me truly believe he's my forever daddy and I'm his perfect naughty boy.

***

Thanks for reading! If you enjoyed Monty and Luke's book, I'd

ALEX SILVER

appreciate it if you left a review to help other readers find their story. And be sure to read about Tate in Service Call available at: www.amzn.com/B09YDNFJ5V

If you're looking for more Summer of Adventures be sure to check out the rest of the series at: https://www.amazon.com/dp/B09D627KGK

Summer of Adventures is a spin off from my contemporary romance series Table Topped available at: https://www.amazon.com/gp/product/B08R6LM6YG

And if you want more kink, check out New Ground, an M/M/X urban fantasy novel with psychic links and daddy kink. www.amzn.com/B08NHQFJDZ

ABOUT THE AUTHOR

Alex Silver (he/them) grew up mostly in Northern Maine and is now living in Canada with one spouse, two kids, and two birds. Alex is a trans guy who started writing fiction as a child and never stopped. Although there were detours through assisting on a farm and being a pharmacist along the way.

Visit me online at:

http://alexsilverauthor.wordpress.com/

Join my Facebook group at:

https://www.facebook.com/groups/alexsalcove

Follow me on BookBub at:

https://www.bookbub.com/profile/alex-silver

Sign up for my newsletter for a free short story at:

https://landing.mailerlite.com/webforms/landing/i2w6l7

And as always, consider leaving a review on Amazon or Goodreads if you enjoyed this book, reviews are of vital importance to independent authors, thanks!

Be sure to explore my entire catalog at Amazon:

More by Alex Silver

Summer of Adventures

Kinky Contemporary Romance

Dungeon Master (M/M)	Book 1	www.amzn.com/B09D9ZTWDK
Knotty Boy (M/M)	Book 2	www.amzn.com/B09D4NG4L7
Service Call (M/M)	Book 3	www.amzn.com/B09YDNFJ5V
Picture Perfect (M/X)	Book 4	www.amzn.com/B09YDN81N7
Puppy Love (F/X)	Book 5	www.amzn.com/B09YFBWCKV
Stud Muffin (M/M/M)	Book 6	www.amzn.com/B0B51XVMGX

Table Topped

Contemporary Romance

Roll for Initiative (M/M)	Book 1	www.amzn.com/B08R6M1XBT
Charisma Check (M/M)	Book 2	www.amzn.com/B08R6J14VZ
Saving Throw (M/NB)	Book 3	www.amzn.com/B08SL3WF2Q
Plus One Bonus (M/X)	Book 4	www.amzn.com/B091V3G8DL
Dump Stat (F/F)	Book 5	www.amzn.com/B0992TD65Y

Hauntastic Haunts

M/M Paranormal Romance

Dan's Hauntastic Haunts Investigates: Goodman Dairy (*Book 1*) www.amzn.com/B07YSV2ZNQ
Dan's Hauntastic Haunts Investigates: Hawk Lake (*Book 2*) www.amzn.com/B081LM3WXP
Dan's Hauntastic Haunts Investigates: Ivarsson School (*Book 3*) www.amzn.com/B087QPR6TD

Drew's Haunted Hangout (*A Hauntastic Haunts Short Story 1*)
Rafael's Haunted Halloween (*A Hauntastic Haunts Short Story 2*)
Lee's Haunted Holiday (*A Hauntastic Haunts Short Story 3*)
Free download links to the shorts are available in my FB group:
https://www.facebook.com/groups/alexsalcove

Psions of SPIRE

Urban Fantasy

Shelter (M/M)	Novella 0.5	www.amzn.com/B07NM9XL8K

ALEX SILVER

Bright Spark (MMMM)	Book 1	www.amzn.com/B07NZ8KPS6
Bold Move (MMMM)	Novella 1.5	www.amzn.com/B07YVGZXDM
Keen Sense (M/M)	Book 2	www.amzn.com/B07R6L8W91
Weak Link (M/M)	Novella 2.5	www.amzn.com/B07T4J2LJZ
Quick Fire (M/X)	Book 3	www.amzn.com/B07VGTF3NB
Clear Sight (M/M)	Book 4	www.amzn.com/B07ZQP7BDS
New Look (M/M)	Book 4.5	www.amzn.com/B08F4GBK63

New Ground (M/M/X)   A SPIREverse daddy kink standalone www.amzn.com/B08NHQFJDZ

Shared Universe Series
Superhero Romance

Super U: Rising Storm (M/X)   Super U Book 1   www.amzn.com/B09FDJJ227

www.ingramcontent.com/pod-product-compliance
Lightning Source LLC
Chambersburg PA
CBHW022023170626
46808CB00003B/1041